I0629962

TRIANGULATION: STEEL CITIES

The 2013 Edition of Parsec Ink's Annual
Confluence of Speculative Fiction

Published in 2015

ISBN: 978-0-9828606-4-9

Cover Art: Karen Yun-Lutz
Editor: Stephen V. Ramey
Layout: Barbara Carlson

Parsec Ink is a subsidiary of Parsec, Inc., a literary organization. For more information, visit our website at www.parsec-sff.org/

Parsec Ink
PO Box 3681
Pittsburgh, PA 15230-3681

Acknowledgements

We gratefully acknowledge substantial financial support from:

**Gordon A. Graves, in memory of his father,
Russell D. Graves, 1907-1988**

We also want to acknowledge the buckets of time and talent donated by our slush pile readers and those who offered advice.

Special thanks to Jamie Lackey for her advice on this project.

Thanks to **Diane Turnshek** for having the courage to create this series and **Barb Carlson**, for editing the anthologies in 2004-05, **Pete Butler** for transforming us to an international, semi-pro paying market during his three years as editor, and for establishing a high bar for quality, **Bill Moran** for continuing that tradition in 2010 and **Jamie Lackey** for stepping up in 2011, and again in 2015.

Finally, let us remember **Ann Cecil** (1940-2011), whose dedication to this cause was unparalleled and constant. Not only did she handle the financial aspects of the anthology, she also coordinated the Parsec Science Fiction and Fantasy Short Story Contest. We miss her.

Table of Contents

Gray Feathers

by Nathaniel Lee

The old man sat on the park bench, feeding the pigeons. He wore a long canvas coat with deep pockets, and his knobby fingers were delicate as they dipped into the red-and-white striped popcorn container and withdrew stale crumbs. The pigeons burbled and hummed around him, their excitement renewed with every meager handful he sprinkled for them. He had a short beard, well-groomed, and a felt hat on the bench beside him. His hair was gray. The wooden bench was gray. The pigeons were gray. The city was gray. It was 1986. Overhead, the sun didn't shine so much as glower through the overcast.

He was in Minnie's spot.

"You're in my spot," Minnie told him.

He looked up and met her gaze. His eyes were dark brown, almost black, stark against his pale face.

"It's okay," Minnie said. "I can sit somewhere else if I have to. But I thought you should know. They were expecting me." She pointed at the pigeons. "That's why there are so many of them."

The old man followed her gesture as if surprised to find pigeons all around him. "Ah," he said. "You are feeding the pigeons here every day?" He had an accent, something sharp and Slavic.

"Yes." Something nudged at the back of Minnie's mind, a rusty and disused rule of etiquette. "I'm Minnie. It's nice to meet you. What's your name?"

"I am Yuri. I am sorry to trouble you." He leaned forward as if to stand, and Minnie suddenly realized that this was the longest conversation she'd had for six months.

"No!" she said. "No, I mean. You…you stay there. You sit there for today. I'll sit over here." She moved to the next bench, seven or eight feet away. "There's lots of pigeons."

Yuri hesitated, half-risen, then dropped back down with a faint grunt. He glanced her way. "Thank you," he said.

"Oh, never you mind." Minnie's voice sounded shrill and slightly panicked, even to her own ears. "Happy to help."

They sat in silence for a time. Across the street, a youth in shiny pants swaggered past with an oversized boombox on his shoulders. Minnie hated those things, but they seemed to be everywhere, blasting out horrible music and attracting crowds of teenagers who spun and flopped on the ground like they were having seizures. Minnie hoped that wouldn't happen now, in her favorite spot for feeding the birds. She tossed out some birdseed and watched the young man until he disappeared. The pigeons drifted toward Minnie, the more familiar face, and she tossed generous handfuls of seed and breadcrumbs to them. More birds arrived, gray wings flapping out of the sky, until the area between Minnie and Yuri was a bobbing sea of round gray heads.

"Do you like pigeons?" she asked, raising her voice to be heard over the rustle and coo of the birds.

Yuri glanced up, startled from some private thought. "I…they are calming, sometimes. Little gray heads, like bullets. We call them the gray ladies, my people, or city angels. They do not care who feeds them; they are happy only to be fed. Many men should be so wise."

His accent intrigued Minnie. He sounded like a Russian. Russians were dangerous and exotic. She'd seen a movie last month about Russians and fighter planes. It had Tom Cruise in it. "I love pigeons. My Frank used to call them 'rats with wings,' but I think they're adorable. I feed them every day." She paused, struggling with a brief internal debate. "Where are you from, Yuri?"

He looked at her with a wry smile and blinked his dark eyes. "I move to this city from Michigan. Before that, Pennsylvania. I live many places because my work, she moves always, always."

"Originally, I mean."

"That is something I wonder about, too," Yuri said. He crumbled a larger piece of bread and sprinkled it on the ground. "I think I have forgotten."

"Oh. I've always lived here."

"In the city?"

"Yes, right here." She pointed. "That's my building. I've lived there for fifty years."

"Ah, so." Yuri blinked his dark eyes at her. "It must be nice to live so long in one place. To have roots. To have family."

"No, no family." Minnie sighed. "Not since my Frank died. No one wants to bother with crazy Aunt Minnie. I get my check from the Social Security office and I talk to my pigeons."

"We are alike, then," said Yuri. "Orphans in a strange land. Forgotten by those who should look after us. It is good, I think, to know that you are not alone in being alone." He glanced around as though looking for someone, but the park was almost empty. No one wanted to get rained on.

"I just worry who will feed my pigeons when I'm gone."

"Responsibility is a terrible burden. I will share yours, if you do not mind, and so we will bear the weight together. Yes?" He stood, his coat rustling around his ankles, and retrieved his hat.

"You'll come back and feed the pigeons?" Minnie blinked.

"Yes. I must wait here, and so I will make myself useful while I can. 'From each according to his ability,' as it is said." Again the almost bitter smile.

"I'll see you tomorrow, then. Yuri." It was almost a question.

"Dasvidanya." Yuri dumped the last scraps of bread from his bag. He folded it with care and tucked it into one of his innumerable pockets. He bowed slightly, oddly formal, and strode stiffly away, his coat billowing behind him and giving him a hunched look.

Yuri was the first man Minnie had ever met who seemed to share her enthusiasm for birds, and his knowledge far outstripped hers, at least in academic terms. He knew about all the different species and had a strikingly exact knowledge of the types of feather and the vagaries of flight. Yuri told Minnie about roller pigeons, the poor inbred strains that could not fly straight and tumbled over and over in midair when they flew, bred to do so by humans who thought them funny and cute. Yuri's lugubrious imitation of a roller pigeon in flight made her laugh and cry all at once. Minnie, in turn, told Yuri about her somewhat specialized knowledge of the personalities and individuals that made up her local flock. She told him the names she had for the leaders among the pigeons, about Turk and Bumper and Pillow-Britches and little Pie-Eye. She showed him the brands of seed they preferred and lectured him about the best way to toss out the food to ensure fair-handed distribution despite Bumper's ardent efforts to keep everything for himself. Minnie hadn't talked so much in years, and she hadn't laughed at all since Frank had passed on.

"It's just so hard," she confessed to Yuri one afternoon. Their relationship had progressed to the point where they could sit on either end of the same park bench without either of them becoming spooked and fleeing, although Yuri tended to crane his neck anxiously and scan the park as if fearful of being observed. "I wonder sometimes what Becca - my niece - is up to. The last I heard, she was married to some doctor type and moved to Texas. Texas! But I don't know her number or her address, and even if I could find it, I couldn't bear to be apart from my babies for the time to take a trip. Do you have any family, Yuri?"

"None that I know of," Yuri said. His voice was raspy today. Minnie hoped he wasn't coming down with something serious. "I am the last. I have heard nothing of my brothers for ... many years."

"How sad. Did they have any children?"

"They may have done, but I cannot know. We were men of action in our youth, fond of danger and thrills. We did many foolish things. Likely they are gone now."

"Everything passes away, doesn't it? Friends and family and all that, and then it just comes down to this." Minnie sighed. "Feeding pigeons."

"It is a noble calling. The birds…they are free, free in a way you and I can never be. They may fly away at any time, and they never lose their way." Yuri shifted restlessly, tugging at the collar of his coat. "I think helping them to fly makes the world a happier place, on balance. It is a better thing than most I have done in my life. I remember…" He coughed, a dry and racking spasm, but waved away her fluttering gestures of concern. "No, no. Do not fear for me. I have earned this, this penalty, this slow death. It is mine as much as anything is. I accept it, now, and I only hope to do some small good before it takes me."

Minnie and Yuri sat a while longer in silence. Minnie struggled against herself and won. "Would you like to come up for tea? I have chamomile, I think. That's supposed to be good for a cough."

Yuri rumbled, deep in his throat, a sound that might have been anger or amusement. "It is unwise."

"Oh, are you allergic?"

He chuckled, then winced and lifted a hand to his chest. "No, unwise for you, little gray lady. Unwise to be close."

"I…I don't…"

"No, no, never mind. I am old, and I say many things that do not make sense, even to me." He heaved himself to his feet. "Come. We will have some tea, yes?"

But his restless black eyes scanned the empty streets, bare now of leaves and waiting for snow, and he did not stay with her in her cramped and crowded apartment long enough to remove his coat.

☼

"I'm worried about Pillow-Britches," Minnie told Yuri as he shuffled to the bench—their bench, now—his head bobbing like a pigeon himself and his back more hunched than ever. "I haven't seen her for days."

"There are many fates that can befall a small pigeon in the city," Yuri said. "I have seen cats lurking in the alleys. Likely they are drawn by the pigeons, as the pigeons are drawn by the bread."

"Oh, you're awful!" said Minnie. "You make it sound as though it's our fault."

"Everything has a price." Yuri shrugged. "Yet we must act, or else what meaning is there to anything?"

"But still…dogs. Cars. Poison. Some people poison the poor birds, did you know?"

"It is a cruel world. What can be done? We might give them their bread, but we cannot be everywhere. We cannot." Yuri stared off into the middle distance, lost in some recollection. He was doing that more and more lately.

"I read an article the other day. A single cat roaming outside can kill ten thousand songbirds per year! Imagine!"

"I have never understood the appeal of the cat to be a pet. They are the last of the truly dangerous beasts, the tigers and the lions. Wolves ate the flocks, not the shepherds, and man killed them all. Bears wished only to be alone and to sleep, and man killed them all. It is the cats who still hunt, and for sport. For play! Your ancestors fled from the lions on the veldt, yet now you keep that lion's many-times grandchildren as idle toys. And those toys kill the pigeons as once they killed men."

"I don't keep them," Minnie said. She pursed her lips. "What can we do for Pillow-Britches, do you think?"

Yuri shook his head. "She knows her way home. All the gray ladies do. She is alive, she will find her way back to you. She is not, she never will. Only can you wait to see. You gave to her your bread, once. You cannot interfere again." He stopped speaking, his lips thinning beneath his tufted beard.

Minnie followed the line of Yuri's gaze. A black car with tinted windows sat parked at the street corner, barely visible in the growing twilight. She couldn't see inside, but there was a red cigarette flare visible briefly through the smoked glass. After a while, Yuri spoke again.

"Always the cats are watching for strays, and we cannot be everywhere."

"Yuri…"

He wasn't looking at her. "I wished to give you a gift. I think I must give it now." Yuri rummaged in his coat, and withdrew a small, dark box. "It is tea from Russia, a good strong tea. It tastes of oranges, and is good for the heart. Here, please," he said, proffering the box. "To repay. To thank, for all you have done."

"I don't understand," said Minnie. She reached a hesitant hand for the box.

Yuri stood, moving with uncharacteristic swiftness. "I must go." He turned and walked away, standing almost upright. His coat rippled as if in a heavy wind, though he kept it wrapped tightly against himself. "Do not follow. Unwise."

"Yuri."

He walked more quickly, pigeons scattering before him.

"Yuri!"

Minnie was short, and her legs ached all the time these days. She scrambled to her feet and hurried as best she could, but Yuri's scarecrow frame rapidly outdistanced her. When she reached the street, he was gone. A soft growl of a motor drew her eyes to the corner, just as the black car purred away down the street. The window cracked, and she saw a cigarette tumble out into the air and burst into a fire-bloom of sparks on the asphalt.

Minnie heard the sound of wings, great flapping noises like someone shaking out a tarp. She looked up, but could see nothing past the light of the streetlamps. Behind her, the pigeons huddled in a cooing mass. Pillow-Britches wasn't there.

Yuri was gone for a long time. Minnie still visited the park, but her trips grew more furtive, more cursory. She felt exposed, walking between the gray buildings with the lowering clouds overhead. She passed through panic and worry into anger, veered into sadness for a bit, and ran a quick detour through anger again before arriving in a new state of fear, a creeping, lingering dread as sourceless as the winds that clutched at her tenth floor apartment. Something unpleasant had happened to Yuri, and she knew deep in her grimy, battle-scarred heart that whatever it was might happen to her, too. Her association with Yuri. His constant wariness. Unwise.

It was with a curious sense of detached fatalism that Minnie opened her apartment door one evening to discover Yuri curled in a ball on her doorstep, his long gray coat pooling on the floor around him. He was emaciated, his gray hair gone white, his skin slack and spotted. His eyes were the same, though, jet-black pools, too dark to distinguish between pupil and iris. Almost no white was showing. His eyes looked like birds' eyes.

"Please," Yuri said. "It is not your fight. But I have no place else. They are…always watching." He held up one clawlike hand to clutch at her layered skirts.

Minnie hesitated for a long time. People bred pigeons and trained them to react the right way, she remembered. People thought pigeons couldn't help themselves. Other people left out poison for them. But some people threw breadcrumbs in the park and cried in the night when a cat ate a broody hen.

Minnie reached down and helped Yuri to his feet.

He could barely stand, but he was lighter than she'd expected, barely there at all. She draped his arm around her shoulders—he was so much taller than she that his legs dragged on the ground—and they shuffled inside.

"A window," Yuri gasped. "See them when they come."

"There isn't a lot of options," Minnie told him. "Come on. I'm putting you in the bedroom.

The radio news was playing clips from recent news when Minnie and Yuri tottered into the bedroom and its towering stacks of cages and sacks of feed. "…tear down this wall…" the President mumbled as Minnie switched off the sound. The silence rolled in like a tide, and she could hear the wind slithering past the windowpanes. Minnie dropped Yuri onto the untidy bed with a grunt and a puff of dust, then arranged his gangly limbs as comfortably as she could. His legs stuck out several feet past the end of the coverlet. Minnie propped them up with a footstool. She tried to shuck him of his damp overcoat, but he shrieked like a wounded animal when she touched it.

"No, please," he said. "I must rest. Only for a moment." His eyes were already closed.

"What happened, Yuri? Should I call the police?"

"No!" his voice grew strong again, just for a moment, though he still did not open his eyes. "No police. No governments. Cat's-paws. The war…the war has come again. Everything will burn. The lake of fire."

"Yuri, you're scaring me," Minnie said. "What happened to you?"

"I remember…flying. But I have forgotten now. I forget so much. The war never ends. Please. I must rest. They know. They know everything. Dark wings. All those years, they knew already. I fall. I flee. They come for me and I cannot flee any further. I have no country. I have no home. I know nothing. I do not think they care anymore." He wheezed a long, difficult breath, then began to cough. "The sky is burning," he said. "Minerva,"—it was the first time he had used her full name—"thank you." Yuri went limp.

Minnie sat for a while in the dark and listened to the wind trying to creep inside. She wondered when she had told Yuri about her proper name, which she had always hated. After a time, she retrieved a fluffy down comforter from the wooden chest beside the bed and draped it over Yuri's slumbering form. Then she made tea. A strong Earl Grey, for wakefulness.

Outside, the wind picked up. The gusts were normally strong here on the upper stories, but from the sound of things, it would be a proper storm soon. Minnie sipped her tea and watched the clock tick the seconds away. After her tea had gone cold, Minnie noticed a sound outside the window, something beyond the rising howl of the wind. A fluttering, as of many wings, and a soft cooing that inveigled itself through the chinks in the walls and the cracks of the windows. Minnie dragged a chair over to the sink and stood on tiptoe to peer out through the small window-vent above it.

On the tops of the buildings and along every windowsill, along the ledges and atop all the signs and light fixtures outside, the pigeons were gathering. The edges of their forms blurred together, creating a single being of bobbing heads and beady black eyes, of tiny, warm bodies and gray-white guano. They lined every available surface all the way down to the street. There, toy-like at this distance, a black car squatted beneath a streetlight. Minnie's eyes could never have been good enough to see such detail, but she could have sworn there was a tiny pinprick of red as someone inside puffed on a cigarette. No birds perched on the car, nor any on the streetlamp above it. As Minnie watched, the rear door opened a crack, and a dark form slunk out.

A cat! They were dumping a cat on the street. She heard the sound of the pigeons turn from a contented murmur to shrill alarm. The cat leapt to the roof of the car, and paused, tail lashing as it stared upwards.

Minnie's eyes narrowed.

The walk from her apartment to the ground was a long one, at least as far as Minnie's aging joints and stubby legs were considered, but she made it in record time, pulling on a puffy overcoat atop her stained blouses and the ragged wool hand-warmers she wore on her arms. Minnie slammed out of the door of her building, armed with a straw broom and a towering rage.

The car was gone. At first, Minnie thought the cat was, too, but then she caught sight of a black blur, heading for the closing apartment door almost faster than her eyes could follow. She swung like a golfer and was gratified to feel a solid hit shiver up the wooden handle as she connected. The cat tumbled away and scampered under a mailbox in fright. It hissed at her from the darkness, its eyes flaring like cigarette ends. Minnie brandished her broom, unwilling to advance into the shadowed street. A standoff.

The cat crawled out and regarded her. It licked a paw and washed one ear, almost contemplatively. Then it leapt, not at Minnie but up, scrambling onto the decorative molding over the door of the building beside hers. It jumped again and again, to a ledge, a cornice, a windowsill. Minnie watched it go, trapped helplessly on the ground. The pigeons fled from its approach, wings whirring up into the night in a gray-feathered cloud. Flight spread like a contagion, rippling along the gathered crowds until the whole city seemed to be filled with the sounds of wings and falling feathers. The sounds did not fade away; instead, they concentrated, spiraling toward one spot in particular.

Somewhere up in the darkness and the wind, Minnie heard glass break.

Running up the stairs so soon after her descent brought Minnie to the brink of collapse, her eyes and nose running, her back trickling with sweat. She'd left the coat three flights down, the broom six. She burst into her apartment with a gasp of pain as her left knee twisted and surrendered. The door to the bedroom was open, and through it she saw the dark hole, the ragged glass, and the curtains thrashing in the wind's terrible grip. She limped forward. There was no glass on the floor; nothing had broken in from the outside, then, though, judging from the layer of feathers and droppings on the floor, quite a few somethings had come in afterward. There were spots of blood on the windowsill, and tufts of black fur that looked to have been torn out by the roots.

The bed was empty, the covers thrown back. Draped across it like a discarded burial shroud was Yuri's gray trenchcoat. In the center, right where Yuri's hunched back should have been, was a single enormous feather, stretching as long as Minnie's forearm. Not white. Not black. Gray, like a pigeon. Minnie picked it up, marveling at its softness.

Outside, the wind faded for a moment, and Minnie heard the sound of wings fluttering in the night. Then the wind returned, and Minnie was alone.

She packed Yuri's coat into the wooden box with the down comforter and the gray feather, sealed in a plastic bag. She took the feather out sometimes when she had tea, or just to look at. The tea was orange and spicy, and good for the heart. She went to the park to feed the pigeons. Pillow-Britches never came back, but Minnie hadn't really expected her to. She cried once or twice, and it made her nose run in the cold. The tea helped with that.

She wondered sometimes which side of the war Yuri had been on. Once, she thought she saw a tall, hunched man stalking across the park in a long coat, but she didn't call out or run after him. Yuri knew the way home, and she suspected he'd remembered how to fly after all. Perhaps the tall man would remember eventually, too, but it wasn't Minnie's place to say anything. Instead, she smiled to herself and tossed another handful of bread crumbs. On the roof of her building, the pigeons nested and cooed, laying eggs and dropping feathers.

No cats ever came there again.

Nathaniel Lee is an author and editor. His short fiction has appeared in dozens of venues online and off, including Nightmare Magazine, Beneath Ceaseless Skies, and Ideomancer. He serves as the fiction editor at both the Escape Pod science fiction podcast and the Drabblecast, where strange stories by strange authors are presented for strange listeners. You can see a full bibliography at his microfiction blog, www.mirrorshards.org, and follow him on Twitter @scattercat.

The Building-King of Pittsburgh

by Jamie Lackey

Cold rain falls on mounds of dirty snow, and gray buildings loom over faded pavement. Cars hiss by, and Tallie huddles in the flimsy shelter of the bus stop, cowering under an oversized, overconfident, two-dimensional lawyer. She dislikes the way he points at her, distrusts the printed promises at his feet, but she can't move away and stay out of the wind. She closes her eyes and tries to forget that he's there.

He's not real, anyway.

She is though, and so is the rain and the cold and the snow.

Overhead, the buildings murmur to each other. They blink their sad window-eyes, and soot seeps down their stone sides like cheap mascara.

They are real, but also not.

"I feel the cold in my foundation," an old skyscraper grumbles.

"The winter of '42 was worse," the hulking courthouse says.

"Everything was worse in '42."

Tallie doesn't remember the winter of '42. She doesn't remember any time when things have been worse.

"The king can help with your foundation," the library whispers. "He helped fix my broken fire escape."

"Shh!" a matronly cathedral with stained glass windows and a barred gate says. "She's listening again!"

"What do we care?" asks a gruff old office building with carved lions flanking its glass doors.

"Well, it's just unnatural," says the cathedral.

"I wish I couldn't hear you," Tallie whispers. While she's at it, she wishes for a cup of coffee, a sandwich, a hot shower, a warm bed, and just for good measure, world peace and a pony.

She gets precisely none of it.

"Imagine that," the cathedral huffs. "She eavesdrops on private conversations, then tries to excuse herself by wishing she was deaf? How utterly low class."

Tallie has never liked the cathedral. "I could put a rock through one of your precious windows," she says.

"You just try it, missy," the cathedral's stones grate as she leans over the street. Her shadow swallows the bus stop. "I will crush you."

"Now, now," says the office building. "She's not the type to cast stones, and we all know it."

The cathedral sniffs, but subsides to her normal place.

"Why don't you come on in," the office building says. "I'm well heated, and my lobby has one of those new-fangled single-cup coffee machines."

"Security will find me," Tallie says. "They'll throw me out."

The office building shrugs. "Maybe. But you can warm up a bit, first. Have some coffee. We might even be able to find you a sandwich."

Tallie wonders if the buildings can read her mind. She glances up at the lawyer on the poster. What if he can read her mind, too? She edges away. His eyes bore into her, brimming with want.

She bolts into the office building.

She makes coffee—two creams and three sugars, the real stuff in the rough brown packets. The elevator dings and hisses open. She ducks behind the couch. "It's fine," the office building says. "I sent it. You can hide in one of the executive offices." The elevator is small, walls lined with deep velvet. Soft. Padded.

"I can't," Tallie says.

"You can trust me."

Tallie does trust him. She likes his lions. She steps into the elevator. The doors close. She gasps in tiny breaths until the doors hiss open again.

"Second door on the left."

There's a beautiful view of the city and a green dress hanging on the back of the door. And a private bathroom.

She stares at the shower. And the thick, soft towels.

Tallie weighs her options. The building offers no advice.

"Do you have eyes to close?" Tallie asks.

"No."

She peels off her clothes. They are heavy with rain, and the layers closest to her skin stink. Goosebumps cover her arms.

The soap smells like roses.

Tallie stands in the shower for a long time, waiting for something terrible to happen. She flinches at every noise. It takes ten minutes to work up the nerve to wash her hair.

The water at her feet turns gray.

She wraps up in one towel and dries her hair with another. She finds a comb and counts 100 strokes, till her tangled hair falls smooth. She rubs scented lotion into her skin. She braids her hair.

The dress fits. She finds unopened panty hose in a drawer, and three pairs of shoes in the coat closet along with a long fur coat. In one pocket, she finds a clean lace handkerchief and a pair of sparkly green earrings.

The building remains silent.

She returns to the bathroom and wipes faded steam off of the mirror. She slides the earrings into her long-empty earlobes. She struggles a bit with the right ear, but they sparkle so beautifully in the low light.

It has been a long time since Tallie has worn anything beautiful.

She stands by the window and looks at her ghost reflection over the city. Three rivers reflect the shimmering lights. Love tugs at her heart. "It's a nice view."

There is a couch against the far wall. She locks the office door and uses the coat as a blanket and an extra towel for her pillow.

"There are sheets in the closet," the building says.

But Tallie's eyes are already closed, and she sleeps.

No one sees her as she leaves the next morning. Their eyes skip over her like she belongs. She stops for another cup of coffee. Someone has brought fresh doughnuts, and she eats one. She licks lemon cream off of her fingers. People smile without meeting her eyes.

"You love this city."

Tallie shrugs. Of course she does.

"You should go see the building-king," the office building says. Tallie's knees shake at the thought, but they're hidden behind her new coat.

Outside, the winter air is cold, but sun peeks through the buildings.

Tallie stops and puts a hand on a stone lion. "Thank you," she says.

The building rumbles.

Tallie's new shoes are simple black flats, and surprisingly comfortable. She strolls down the streets and sips her coffee. She watches pigeons move in iridescent feathered waves and lets the ocean of foot traffic pull her along.

She arrives at a square surrounded by turret-topped glass walls. The building-king of the city. He regards her.

She sits at a table where someone has abandoned half of a bagel. She shares it with the pigeons.

"I would repair our city I have need of subjects," the king says. Its voice is deep, and Tallie can feel its rumble in the sidewalk.

Tallie watches the pigeons. "Did you do this to me?"

"No. But I can use you, if you're willing."

Tallie strokes her fur coat and finishes her coffee. She thinks about wishes, then about world peace and a pony.

It has been a long time since she worked. She misses functioning.

"What will it cost?"

"The more you interact with us, the less they will see you."

Tallie thinks about eyes sliding past her. She's already lonely. No one will miss her.

The king's glass walls are beautiful in the morning sunlight.

"What do I do?"

☼

She carries messages and magic for the building-king. The magic curls around her bones, crackles at her wrists. It is uncomfortable. He sends her uphill, away from the steel towers and hulking fortresses. She walks on cracked sidewalks, and the buildings around her weep. They mourn their crumbling porches, their cracked foundations.

Some are too far gone to cry. The dead buildings pull at Tallie's heart. She wonders how long it will take for the whole neighborhood to fall silent. She wonders if the building-king can stop it.

She wonders if she can help.

She reaches the YMCA. Its sign flickers, but the building greets her. "Welcome, welcome! Yours is a new face! Do come in!"

Tallie sits on its cold steps and turns her face to the weak sun. "I have a message."

The YMCA trembles with anticipation.

"The king is pleased with you."

"I—I didn't even know he knew about me."

"You do good work. Spread cheer in this sad place. You're a place of learning and safety. He sends this reward."

Tallie presses both hands to the concrete steps. She feels distant and dizzy and very hot. Her bones tingle. Then the moment passes, and the cold wind sweeps the feeling away.

The changes to the YMCA are subtle. Its sign glows steadily now, and tiny cracks and fissures have sealed.

"Thank you," the YMCA says. "Please come in. Have some coffee."

Tallie sits in the computer lab and watches videos of running ponies. She watches their babies take trembling first steps. The man at the computer next to her smiles at her. She reads an article about mental illness, then one about the history of downtown.

She wonders how much of what she sees is real.

The building-king sends her to every corner of the city. Busses stop for her now. They make low purring noises when she sits, and the drivers never see her. She sleeps in a different building every night. They seem happy to have her.

Laundromats supply her with new clothes, and the ever-present hunger slowly fades as kitchen after kitchen opens up to her.

She is proud of the help she gives. Proud to be the building-king's messenger. Human eyes ghost over her in a different way now. It is both better and worse.

She cries when she repairs a crack in the kind office building's lion. "Thank you," she whispers.

He opens his doors, and she sips coffee while he tells stories about his youth.

"Don't think I don't know what you're doing," the cathedral says the next morning.

"What do you mean?" Tallie asks.

"You fix his lion. That tiny, stupid crack did the beast even need a tail, honestly? And you ignore my broken window. You're holding a grudge, and I don't appreciate it."

Tallie hasn't noticed the window, and the building-king hasn't mentioned it. He hasn't given her any magic for the cathedral.

"Let me in," Tallie says.

The cathedral sniffs, but her gate creaks open and her heavy wooden door groans. Tallie slips inside. Early morning sunlight paints colors on the far wall, except for one ragged, sun-drenched spot. Tallie's footsteps echo on the marble floors. She kneels in that spot of un-colored sun and presses her palms to the floor.

The feeling is familiar now, but harder, since the magic comes from inside her. Something wrenches open in her, and the light turns purple.

Her knees buckle. She collapses on the floor.

The cathedral is silent for a long moment. "Thank you, child."

Tallie nods. Her skull aches and her joints feel loose and wobbly. She thinks of running ponies.

"You are safe here," the cathedral says.

A woman pushes through the heavy door. She walks within an inch of Tallie's leg. "Keep my daughter safe," she says. "I'd give anything to see her again."

The cathedral sighs. "This woman comes every week," she says. "I do wonder if she'll ever find the girl."

Tallie stares at her mother. Her throat aches. "I don't think so," she whispers.

The building-king gleams his approval from a thousand silver-black windows. "You did not have to help her," he says.

"Then it wasn't a test?" Tallie asks.

The building-king rumbles. "Not one to pass or fail. One for you to see into yourself."

Tallie watches a flock of pigeons explode into a gray-rainbow cloud. She thinks about her mother. "I haven't been happy with what I see in myself for a long time."

"Perhaps you were looking in the wrong places."

Tallie leans back and gazes at buildings in the city skyline. They are her family, and she will take care of them. "Can I ask for one thing?"

The building-king winks his agreement.

"I don't like the lawyer posters. The ones on the bus stops."

The building-king laughs, and the lawyer disappears. Tallie's not sure if he's really gone, or if she just can't see him.

It doesn't matter.

The building-king fills her with magic, and she sets off to help fix the city.

Jamie Lackey lives in Pittsburgh with her husband and cat. Her fiction has appeared in *Daily Science Fiction*, *Beneath Ceaseless Skies*, and the Stoker Award-winning *After Death*…. She's a member of the Science Fiction and Fantasy Writers of America. Her short story collection, *One Revolution*, is available on Amazon.com, and her debut novel, *Left Hand Gods*, is forthcoming from Hadley Rille Books. Find her online at www.jamielackey.com.

A Holiday Romance

[with moonlight, violins, and the whole shebang]

by Pierre Pelot

[translated from the French by Michael Shreve]

Rom sighed and stretched, cracking his knuckles as he stood. His body felt tired, a good tired, as if steeped in a kind of cottony suit.

It had been a hard day, not easy, full of pitfalls, but Rom and his clients had pulled through pretty well. Almost all of his clients. Because there was this Vulk, of course … And shit, Rom thought, it's his own fault. Not my problem.

He had told them and repeated it a hundred times: watch out in this sector, don't go wandering off, stay roped close together, dick to ass, kids, dick to ass (one thing the clients appreciated more than anything, apparently, was this kind of crude banter in the coarse language of Outside: it made them laugh. Even the cold fish, after a while, would be smiling). He had drummed this advice into them and then wouldn't you know it, this jerk Vulk wanted to get smart, and he boldly went and stuck his face on a nasty piece of jutting iron. That was it. Good God, that spot was dangerous. And it wasn't like they hadn't been warned over and over again!

Didn't matter. Except for this Vulk, everything was going fine. A great ascent. Out of five clients at the start, three were left, including Vulk.

And they had just reached the 330th level. Less than seventy floors to go. The biggest dangers were past. Seventy floors could be done in two or three stages, max. A walk in the park.

Rom left the campsite, a room with three straight walls and a missing fourth, and took a few steps through a ruined archway into the hallway. The cement floor was strewn with all kinds of junk and trash, some of which reeked horribly. He stopped at the ridge overlooking the chasm. This was where they had come up, a black hole where you could barely see more than ten feet down. The rest was drowned in shadows and fog.

Rom pissed calmly over the edge. The urine stream sang over unseen protrusions. He shook two or three times while thinking about something else, pulled up the zipper of his suit, and returned to the campsite. The tent was set up on this side of the room, as far from the missing wall as possible. The wall had fallen down a mighty long time ago, leaving an opening onto the void. Another chasm, but this one was certainly more impressive than the shaft they had scaled all day. You could lean over the edge of the cliff here: no way to see the bottom. Because of the mist and the fumes, especially. Some clients preferred the mist because it partly hid the dizzying drop. For others it was the opposite, encouraging an even worse fear of heights. For Rom, it was a laugh. He was a child of Outside, born in the Mountains.

Seven or eight feet up, some fallen plaster formed a kind of awning, a forty- or fifty-foot square protective roof. Rom had made sure the awning was solid (it was probably the remains of a stairway landing or something like that) and set up the bivouac underneath so they would be sheltered from the wind that sometimes screamed through the Dings, and also from the rain that could start falling at any time. Generally, clients did not like the wind and even less so the rain. They were not used to it—and even for those looking for exotic thrills at any price, rain and wind were only good for a little while. Especially the rain.

Rom stepped into the light given off by the lamp sitting on the floor and by the helmet lights. Liottie looked up. Her eyes were worried behind the transparent mask that covered her face. The filter cap over her mouth was an absolutely unbeautiful, lumpy outgrowth. These stupid masks, Rom yelled inside his head. He absent-mindedly scratched his cheek, covered with sparse, scruffy beard. And if you, too, for one reason or another had to wear a protective mask someday, Rom? Never. Impossible. Impossible to go through life with this kind of shitbag on your head. How would you kiss a girl, huh? Rub your filter cap against hers? He wondered if Outsiders needed protection to visit Inside. And then he wondered if Outsiders ever visited Inside, or snuck in, maybe. Anyway, he knew no one who did. Visiting was a one-way street: From Inside to Outside. That's all.

The cream of Society lived Inside, under shelter. With all possible advantages. Outsiders muddled through, trying to live as long as possible. They were there, for example, to guide the Moles on their holidays or to murder them. They were there to dig through the shit.

"How's it going?" he said to Liottie, mainly to hear himself speak.

"Not too well," Liottie said.

I don't give a damn, Rom retorted to himself.

His pale blue eyes fixed on the girl's even paler blue eyes. Good God of the Dings, those eyes! That face, so white, so fine and soft (that was sure!) behind the mask, that body whose curves were so shapely in the protective suit … It was not the first time that Rom had wanted to screw a client—and he never missed an opportunity!—but not like this, not in this way. Liottie was different. Not only did he get butterflies when he looked at her, but, to boot, he caught himself red-handed in tender daydreams, hungering for a cuddle, a caress, kisses and scents. He wanted to sit in a corner with her and talk, listen, maybe just hold her hand. What a bunch of crap, huh?

And that was why Rom was feeling so good, so powerful and fragile at the same time. Indestructible and vulnerable to the max.

"I don't think he's going back down," Liottie said, looking at the body of Vulk lying on the ground. She was talking about him, obviously, and it was about him that she had said, 'Not too well'.

Vulk was young, maybe fifteen or sixteen. This was probably his first time off, his first vacation. And his last, Rom thought. He knelt next to Liottie to look interested in Vulk's fate. His knee rubbed against hers. He felt a tingle like a real electric shock. His eyes met Liottie's again. Behind the preoccupied expression on her face a smile flashed—and she did not move her knee. A victory cry exploded in Rom's head. He felt himself burning up.

"I told him, damn it, to take it easy," he said, trembling his voice a bit, which could have come from anger or from concern for a croaking client.

Vulk was croaking. Absolutely.

Poor little bastard, Rom thought. He told himself he would never take such a young client again. The young ones are completely crazy, they think they can climb anything, smarter than everyone else … and whack! The first chance they get, they trip up or stick their face on a piece of iron like that. And that's it, they die. And Rom couldn't care less. He was there to guide them, not save them.

On the other side of the stretched-out body, the third client, Named, was hugging his knees against his chest. "We did what we could," he muttered. When neither Rom nor Liottie seemed to have heard him, he added, "Really. We tried everything."

Rom cast a blurry eye on him, nodded slowly, and said, "For sure, Named."

"Really," Named repeated.

Then he stayed quiet, grabbed his pack, and opened it. He prepared a nutrition syringe and stuck the needle into the rubber nozzle hanging under the filter cap of his mask. He sucked and swallowed as he slowly pushed in the plunger.

The guy could eat for four. He did not say ten words all day and barely stayed awake during breaks. He was disciplined, obedient, competent and knew relatively well how to deal with ropes and grapples. And old, Rom thought with a feeling bordering on respect ... Named had been around at least thirty years. He knew the Dings. It wasn't his first climb.

That was one thing the moles had going for them: there were a damn lot of them who reached thirty. Old age existed among them. Rom felt no particular envy about this. It was an observation only.

A crazy idea crossed his mind. What if the government was authorizing the moles' jaunts Outside to keep a kind of balance, to give a little helping hand to Death? The accident factor was pretty much banished from life Inside, right? They had to balance things out a little, didn't they? They still had to die someday, in some other way than getting worn out naturally.

He had a certain idea of life Inside from having asked his clients. He had listened to them. He knew that down there the government organized damned publicity campaigns for vacations Outside. Back to nature and that crap.

All of a sudden Vulk stirred, yanking Rom out of his thoughts. He told himself again, very quickly, that in spite of everything (in spite of that hope for a double-long life and all the possible comforts he could imagine) he wouldn't switch his life for a mole's for all the uranium on Earth. Shit, he'd rather croak at twenty-five after a hell of a good time.

"God," Liottie said.

Named stopped nursing his nozzle for the few seconds it took Vulk to give up the ghost. A brief silence followed before Named slammed the syringe plunger and took a big gulp of nutriment.

"Okay," Rom said.

"We tried everything," Liottie murmured. "Named and I put together our rust-gum to try and fix the tear in his mask, but it was too big."

"You should get it back," Rom said as gently as possible, trying not to show his irritation. He was a guide, not a nanny. "If either of you gets snagged, you'll need that gum."

Since the two clients were not budging, he leaned over Vulk's corpse and plucked off the rust-gum. The skin of the mask pulled up with it before dropping back to reveal the tear that had poisoned the bum. That's the price you pay, poor moles, he told himself. That's the price you pay for coming to breathe our rotten air when you're safe down there in the sterilized depths.

He folded the strips of rust-gum and slipped them into one of his pockets. "Okay." And he grabbed Vulk by the ankles to drag him off.

Liottie slapped her hand around his wrist. "You're going to …? What do you figure on doing with him?" Her voice got carried away by her emotions.

Have you ever seen such a beautiful girl, old Rom? No kidding! She's maybe twenty years old, no more. Yes, old pal. Woman personified, and with those siren eyes.

Very calmly he asked, "Is this your first climb, Liottie?" He knew the answer. Liottie and he had talked a lot in previous bivouacs. She had done Ding 32 and the southern face of Ding 07, a real nasty piece of work! She knew the Mountains, and when she talked about climbing a Ding (not just a third-class Build, but a first or second-class Frame-Carcass) she knew what she was talking about.

She lowered her eyes, took her hand off Rom's wrist. "But he was so young."

So what? Three years younger than me or thereabouts. But he had to go clowning around, that's all. And the idiots didn't bring spare masks!

Rom dragged the body toward the archway. The corpse's outstretched arms raked up some of the plaster debris and rocks. Rom had to stop and fold Vulk's arms over his belly before hauling him onto the landing. The mouth of the vertical shaft gaped two feet away. Rom pushed the body to the edge. At the last second, he hesitated, and then just let it lie there, turning it to face the wall. He went back to the bivouac.

Named had finished eating. He was rolled up in his inflated blanket, probably already asleep.

Rom sat next to Liottie. She looked at him questioningly.

"No," he said. "I left it on the edge."

He fished two tabs of Broy & Broy from a pocket and started chewing. The tabs always had the same disgusting flavor, but it was the only food possible on the go. He dreamed of wild cat stew, really greasy, or the spicy rat skewers that they served in the Jull Jethro restaurant down in the Valley.

"Is he going to … rot?" Liottie asked.

Rom glanced at her. She was still shaking a little, but the emotional shock was fading. She was getting her balance back, and even smiled in an embarrassed excuse-me way when she asked the question.

"Maybe he'll rot, maybe he'll be picked up by Vultures."

She gazed through the archway. "Of course."

"Of course," Rom said. He placed another nut tab on his tongue. Wrapped in his blanket Named stirred and sighed.

After a short while, Liottie asked, "Are there Vultures on this Ding?"

Rom nodded slowly. "There are Vultures on all the third-class Dings because they're the hardest ones to get up. That trap your friends fell into—that first one a few days ago—was probably the work of Vultures." He paused. "Plus, just like Vulk, they paid for their recklessness. They shouldn't have gone off the marked path. They wouldn't have tripped up."

"I've never seen a Vulture," Liottie said.

Rom tried to probe her eyes to see whether or not she was sorry. "They're like all the others," he said. "I mean Outsiders. The few cops who still wander around the Valley gave up chasing after them on the Dings a long time ago. They say there're also Vultures by the Sea. I don't know."

"And in the Country?"

"Not that I know of. In the Country there are too many cops at work. That's what they say."

"Rom, do you know any?"

"Vultures?"

Liottie batted her eyelids. She turned off her helmet light. Rom did the same. The dark and the stinking mist enveloped them. Rom shivered.

"A few, sure," he said. "They generally leave us alone and build their traps out on the edges. After all, we're the ones bringing their prey. That's why I've told you over and over not to wander off the path, to stick by me." And he added, "I don't want you to end up on some Vulture's plate."

There's no better declaration than that, right, old Rom?

In the darkness he could not see Liottie's face, only a vague, pale spot. She stayed silent for a moment, before whispering, "I don't want to either."

Are you going to take that for a yes to your semblance of a declaration, Rom?

Liottie pulled her knees up to her chest. Her hip touched Rom's.

Oh! God of the Dings, Rom...

Before them was the missing wall, the void. A cool draft glided over Rom's flushed face.

Take her in your arms, old boy. You're almost positive that she's waiting for nothing else. They're all like that, all of them, you've never failed, not once! They're on vacation, out of their strict, regulated world, they're at a party! Besides the lure of exoticism, right? Getting it on with a Guide, a Savage from Up There, a Natural from Outside! They all dream of it, they're dying for it, it's an experience worth chalking up for a woman's Lifestyle Inside. Yeah. All of them.

How many times had he pulled down the hermetically sealed zipper on the bottom of a female client's climbing suit? Making sure, of course, not to screw up their protective mask. How many times had he heard them moaning behind their filter caps? Shit, Rom, do it!

The first time he saw Liottie, didn't she have this desire deep down in her eyes? Really? Did she? He didn't know. That's exactly why it's not the same. She, she's not …

She's not what, Rom? Would you have to force yourself to get a hard-on, or what?

Liottie's gentle voice broke the spell. "How many levels to the summit?"

"Seventy," Rom said. His voice cracked. There was a knot in his throat.

"You know this Ding pretty well, don't you, Rom?"

I can't believe it! Rom thought. He felt sapped now, just the idea of hearing his name pronounced by this girl from Inside. It was unreal, this feeling, it had never happened to him before. Never. Not like this.

What's she got that the others don't, Rom? A head in a mask and an ass and breasts and a soft squeezing cu… Okay, Rom, it's not working. It's not by being crude that you'll figure it out. She's got that she's sweet, that's it, she's got you desiring, got you wanting to kiss her pure white skin. She's got, in the fucking name of God, you wanting to keep her with you forever, and sleep next to her without even touching her, and listen to her when she talks, and live with her, forever. FOREVER. That's it. She's got you wanting it to last as long as possible. That's it. She's got you really wanting not to croak when you're twenty-five years old. To create an Outside that's under shelter, too, a burrow, something, an island, some nest, but UNDER SHELTER.

Liottie leaned into him. "You know this Ding, don't you, Rom?"

"Yes," Rom answered. "You could say I was born on it." In the shit of the Valley around the rat farms. In the pretty red smoke that rises over the fields of filth, in the fog, that damned fog that's fatal to your Insider bronchial tubes, but that I've been breathing since I first started wailing between my mother's thighs.

"It's one of the biggest," Rom said.

"I know," Liottie said. "I've been training since my first vacation. I wanted to do Ding 08 precisely because it's one of the biggest. Because at the summit …"

"What?" Rom said.

"Because at the summit, they say, you're on top of the sea of fog and you can see the sky. For real."

"It's true," Rom said. And there you go! That's it! Roost up there with her, just the two of you, nothing but you and her, watching the sky. If you get lucky the mists and vapors might even let a ray of sunlight through.

Liottie was curled up in her inflated blanket (Rom had helped her close the sleeping bag) and had closed her eyes. To find the Guide's face immediately etched on the inside of her eyelids. Her entire body, from head to foot, shivered. The itch that she knew all too well stimulated her nipples.

Rom.

He was so young, so beautiful! A little thin, maybe, but it was completely different than the thinness of the men Inside.

Life Outside was completely different than life Inside. The last animals, that's what they were! (Are Vultures to be classed among the animal kingdom or among the Humans?) Rom, an animal ... And it was terribly exciting. Even more than that. Something else, too.

This was not the first time that she had wanted to give herself to a Guide. She had done it, often, and was never disappointed. Great memories for killing time Inside.

This is stupid, Liottie told herself. I'm from a different class. We have nothing in common. He has this incredible chance to live in communion with Nature and I ... I pay for my social class in my cell in the city, Inside, under the poisoned surface. He breathes this air without a mask, this corrosive air that's going to kill him in a few years. It's stupid.

To reach the summit and see the sky. To see it for real, not just on a telespect screen.

She opened her eyes. Rom's face was there, leaning over her. She saw his eyes in the dark—she saw his smile, a little uncertain, really boyish, almost babyish, as if he was asking himself ... as if he didn't really dare to ...

Nothing like the other Guides who screwed with almost no foreplay and no manners. Nothing like those scheduled sessions of sextherapy Inside.

With a trembling hand she opened her sleeping bag and Rom slipped inside. He was burning hot. He hugged her tightly for a long time before fumbling around between her legs and getting frustrated with the zipper of her suit.

No, not an animal.

ROM.

Nothing at all like anything she had known before. Brought tears to her eyes—and that was super annoying under her mask.

And it was marvelous. MAR-VEL-OUS.

One thing was sure: he would remember the 330th level of Ding 08 for a long time.

He had made love to her like a real jackass—he had certainly made out better the first time he slept with one of the whores at Jethro's restaurant.

Makes you wonder how she could have liked it.

But she did like it. He wanted to believe that: he wanted to convince himself that he had seen it in her eyes the next morning.

The coolest thing, the weirdest thing was that he liked it too. Liked it TER-RIBLY. He knew that he had made out like some savage bum, but he liked it.

Damn!

He was thinking of only one thing: to start up again. He knew that they would start up again. But not just anywhere, not just anytime. Up there.

Up there.

On the summit, on the 400th level of Ding 08, the biggest building carcass on the savage surface, the tallest peak of what had become their Mountains.

Up there.

He knew Liottie tacitly agreed. So, they climbed. Feverishly. They were thinking about nothing but the summit, both of them, and they were putting all their strength into the ascent.

Result: they got up forty levels the next day. When they put their foot on the meager platform of the 370th (part of a little balcony), they were literally worn out. Named looked like he had lost several pounds and he was so pale he was almost transparent.

They stayed roped together as Rom hammered some pitons into a crack in the concrete wall and then snapped the security hooks into the rings.

"Thirty levels left," he said while chewing on his Broy & Broy tabs.

Liottie and Named sucked on their syringes.

"Thirty levels for tomorrow," Rom said.

They were cramped on this tiny platform and had hung their bags on a piece of rusted metal that jutted out of the wall—the remains, maybe, of a steel support beam from the balcony. The void was swirling around below them in the mass of fog and fumes. Beyond the shifting screen they could see the distant, jagged outlines of other peaks, other ding frames. An impressive sight, terrible and magnificent. Poignant.

"I don't think I can do it," Named said. "I must be getting old."

I was hoping so, Rom thought, exchanging a quick glance with Liottie.

"I can wait here, what do you think?" Named asked.

"As you wish," Rom answered. He thought, afterward, that he maybe should have tried a little to convince him that he wasn't as old as that.

They slipped into their inflatable blankets under their safety harnesses and side by side, huddled together on the meager surface of the concrete overhang, they watched night fall. Liottie's hand in Rom's.

And then afterward? Rom thinks.

How stupid! She'll go back to her City under the surface. She's a girl from Inside, shit! Unable to live Outside! There's absolutely no way she can contend with this Nature that she's searching for and you know it. A matter of adaptation? A matter of biochemistry, yes! Ask a goddamn rat to fly …

Too bad!

Too bad … what's too bad?

She'll leave for her City, for her cell, for her comfort and her work, for her telespect and her friends. (Do they have friends down there?) For her sextherapies every day or every week or … She'll see her family again (they have families down there! Not "clans" or "groups", but families, yeah!) and they'll ask her if she had a good vacation, how was it up there on Ding 08, what was the real light like? And all that crap, right.

Too bad! Too bad! Too bad!

Poor Outsider bastard, poor bastard of Nature and dark Fumes and Radiation and Fog. Poor bastard.

And then afterward? Liottie thinks.

Afterward, how stupid! He'll continue his life of a wild thing (but it's not mean to say "wild thing", quite the contrary …), he'll continue his climbs and his conquests, for sure. He'll get tanner and tanner, maybe get in fights in the dive bars at the foot of the dings among the rat farmers and shit diggers. He'll leave and fade away into the yellow and red mists of Nature. He's from Nature, he knows how to fight and live in it—he knows everything you've forgotten. He possesses this lost wealth. He might even know the forests, who knows? He knows all the traps and how to avoid them …

Too bad!

Why too bad?

Or what? Bring him back with you, of course? Like they sometimes bring back a living rat in a cage or a beetle—so that he'll die fast in the purified air, in the normal air. Or maybe to keep him in an airtight container? A sealed suit? And then what, come on?

Not to mention the official ban, the flagrant impossibility to mix, Inside, two such different species as a Natural and a Protected …

Come on, just try to live like a fish out of your aquarium.

Poor little Insider tramp. Poor tramp caught God knows how in the net of one of the countless traps of Outside. Exactly.

Poor stupid jerk.

Cuddled up to each other, huddled together on the concrete cliff. Liottie's hand in Rom's. Yes.

"We made it," Rom said.

He helped Liottie step onto the top of the 400th level of Ding 08.

He repeated, "We made it." They were—pretty much—the first words he had spoken all day and he could think of nothing more original.

They had climbed the last thirty levels without a minute of rest. In a kind of trance. They had made it through some tight spots—like that bitch of a glass wall riddled with razor-sharp shards; that spot alone had required hours of precarious effort; it was not the time for Liottie to tear her suit or mask. And then that last shaft whose plastered walls flaked off in huge slabs under their spiked boots.

"We made it," Rom had said.

Liottie took a few steps on the vast esplanade of cracked concrete. She dropped her bag and her grappling hook. She looked, with her eyes wide open, with her being wide open. She looked at the magnificent landscape that stretched out around her.

The summit of Ding 08 jutted up almost fifty feet above the sea of red fog. And this cottony, bloody fog extended as far as the eye could see, boundless. A few hundred yards to the left another ding summit burst through the stagnant sea, jagged and crowned with twisted girders.

And then the sky above. A gray sky streaked with languid scars of cloud. Much of the sky was very dark.

"Over there," Rom said behind Liottie, "the sun is setting." He was pointing to a point in the red mists, a point that was maybe a little redder than elsewhere, but it needed a practiced eye to tell the difference.

"The sun," Liottie repeated. "The sky. Clouds."

She turned to face Rom. She was teary-eyed and laughing at the same time.

"Oh God," she cried out.

When she threw herself into his arms, he hugged her tightly. His heart was going crazy and he kissed her protective mask, searching for her lips like a jerk, searching for her lips and finding only this goddamn shitty filter cap that almost broke his teeth.

"It's … it's so beautiful!" Liottie said.

She tore herself away from him to look at the sight again, to take it all in. Since she looked like she was about to take off and run all over the esplanade, he yelled, "Watch out! It's full of holes and open shafts!"

She stood still and watched.

She watched the spectacle offered by Nature, this forgotten Foreign Land. She watched the cottony fumes and perpetually dark fog that had covered the surface for dozens and dozens of years. She watched the crazy swirling and curling whose scent she could not breathe in for even a split second without passing out and then dying because she wasn't an Outsider like Rom, because she wasn't condemned to die young like him. She watched the clouds roll by and that invisible point in the sea of smoke where Rom had said that the ever-invisible sun was setting. She asked if the sun was sometimes visible behind the clouds and he said no, of course not. He added that (this was strange) they had a better chance of seeing the glow of the moon sometimes. She watched the summit of the nearest Ding. She watched.

It was the highest climb and it was fantastic, especially being with Rom. She had never been so steeped in the exhalations of rediscovered Nature.

She watched night fall.

☼

They made love several times in a row, but in no hurry. Like never before.

And several times Rom knocked his teeth against her damn filter cap—which was there at the right time to remind him who she was and who he was.

It was chilly. At one point, like he had said, between two inky black clouds they could see a faint, pale glow.

"There you go," Rom whispered, "You even get moonlight."

It was almost as if the whistling wind down below among the shattered steel structures of the buildings, almost as if this song, absolutely doleful in fact, sounded like violins … No kidding.

"The moon," Liottie murmured, hugging Rom. "They're up there and on the Mars colony too."

"Who?"

"The Rulers."

"They're not Inside, down below?" Rom asked. "Aren't there some in your City too?"

"I don't know."

Then again Rom didn't give a damn. He was fighting against an infernal sadness that was perversely worming itself into him.

"And the Sea?" Liottie asked. "Have you seen the Sea?"

He said no. He was from the Mountains. "Maybe I'll go someday, if I have time." He knew very well that he wouldn't have time. The Sea—he cared about it as little as he cared about rat farming or about Liottie's job (which was making a piece of some machine numbered 00089765, which is what she'd told him but she couldn't say anything more because she didn't know anything more), he cared about it as little as he did about the Vultures and the cops in the Country, or about Named who was waiting on the balcony. He didn't care about anything. He simply wanted to kiss Liottie on the lips and that was the one thing he couldn't do.

To kiss Liottie on the lips, plus make love to her and then live with her until the end. There you go. Certainly the most beautiful idiocy he could ask for.

"I went there," Liottie said softly. "Once. On my first vacation—the first time Outside. First you have to get across miles and miles of garbage and mud with a Sea-Guide. Then there's the water under the red fog. That's all." She put her hand on Rom's bare thigh and added, "Nothing compares with the Mountain. There's nothing better than Ding 08."

Rom swallowed hard. He was suddenly cold. He thought: nothing compares with Liottie.

This damn wave of sadness rolled its shredded foam throughout his being. Weighing him down. He wasn't really unhappy, seeing that there was an unparalleled joy pulsing through him at the same time—he was TERRIFICALLY unhappy …

He hesitated and then as if they had a life of their own the words came pouring out of his knotted throat, "Will you come back?"

Stupidity.

He knew it.

Pierre Pelot is a French author of over 200 books. One of the great storytellers of our time, for more than forty years his multifaceted talent has traversed science fiction, thrillers, horror, fantasy and more. His works have been adapted to both the big and small screen and been awarded numerous prizes. Translations of his novels *But What If the Butterflies Cheat?* and *The Child Who Walked On The Sky* have been published by Black Coat Press. He can be found on the web at:

http://www.pierrepelot.fr/pierre_pelot_la_taniere/accueil.html

- - - - - - - - - - -

Michael Shreve has published dozens of works, both fiction and non-fiction. He can be found on the web at www.michaelshreve.wordpress.com.

Samhain Night

by Eric Leif Davin

When we got to the avenue, it was already crowded. Both sides were jammed with parents and their kids. And both parents and kids were in costumes: ghosties and ghoulies of all kinds ran up and down the sidewalks, chasing each other with screams of delight, flitting amongst and between clumps of people. The chatter of the crowd filled the air with excited anticipation. Workers at the Starbucks pushed back the accordion glass panels to open the entire front of the coffee shop to the sidewalk. One of the baristas stepped outside and looked at the crowd. "Wow!" he called over his shoulder to his fellow baristas. "There's a lot more than for the Columbus Day Parade. We'll be busy tonight!" The Columbus Day Parade through the heart of Bloomfield, Pittsburgh's Little Italy, was one of the biggest in the country. But the Steel City's Samhain Night Parade was even bigger. People turned out in hordes to see the guest marchers, who came from their fabulous lands of origin on this night alone.

Nita and I had gotten to the avenue early in order to find a place in the front ranks of viewers, but we were too late. People already lined the avenue four or five deep. We found a vacant storefront stoop and climbed up on the steps to see over the heads of the people. The night carried a slight chill, but it was dry. Only a few thin clouds floated across the dark sky, their long fingers sliding across the leering face of the full yellow moon above. Sprinkled across the night were the brilliant diamond glints of a thousand stars. It was a perfect Samhain Night.

Then, far down to our left, we heard the banging of drums. "Here they come!" someone called, and heads craned as people peered down the dark boulevard. "It's the zombies!"

We stood on tiptoe and, in the distance, we saw the zombie band coming, beating and banging on drums and clanging cymbals discordantly. It took some time for them to reach us, because they shambled slowly. Two stumbling zombies in rotting rags came first, carrying a long banner stretched between: Zombie Marching Drum Band. Except that none of them marched. They staggered and lurched, banging and clashing their instruments to some tune known only to themselves. The banner was right about it being a drum band, though. None of the zombies carried horns of any kind, because none of them had any breath with which to blow them.

They shambled past, to be followed by a contingent of mummies. The mummies tended to stagger and lurch, also, but at least they didn't have rotting flesh hanging from their bones. They were mummies, after all, so where it could be seen beneath their wrappings, their dry brown skin was as brittle as parchment. But they, too, were all percussion, as they had no more breath for wind instruments than did the zombies. Some of them waved to the crowd, their bandages floating from their arms like white streamers in the moonlight.

Next came a troupe of dancing skeletons, their bony feet clattering on the pavement. Some carried xylophones strung from their necks which they pounded with thighbones, others played marimbas. The clattering of their bones mixed with the marimbas and xylophones into a cacophony of syncopated rhythm and the crowd began bouncing and swaying with the beat of the bones.

And then came the Headless Horseman, prancing and dancing on his midnight black steed. The stallion's hooves struck sparks from the pavement and fire blasted in jets from its flaring nostrils. And, inside the jack o'lantern head of the Horseman, more fire burned. The flames lapped out of his eyes and jagged grin as his dark steed reared on its hind legs. The Headless Horseman waved to the crowd like the Lone Ranger. The crowd answered with a chorus of cheers and wild applause.

Then came a pack of satyrs and nymphs. The nymphs danced in gossamer gowns as the satyrs blew on their Pan pipes. The sound of the shrill syrinxes mingled into a swirling, mesmerizing call to panic and wild abandon. One goat-footed satyr caught up a nymph in a diaphanous gown and pranced down the avenue with her thrown over his shoulder, his horned head thrown back in laughing pleasure.

After them came the Civil War vets, who actually marched in unison, their blue wool uniforms worn and torn from slogging through hell on earth and hell down below. At their head was the color guard carrying Old Glory, shot full of bullet holes from a thousand battles on a thousand battlefields, but still flapping bravely in the night breeze.

Just as they reached a spot in front of us, the vets stopped. At an order from their captain they swung their guns to their shoulders. Their captain gave a further order and the Billy Yanks fired a thunderous volley into the night sky. Tongues of fire and clouds of blue smoke erupted from the muzzles of their guns. As the smoke drifted and thinned over the crowd, the vets pulled out their ramrods and, in unison, reloaded their guns. They shouldered them and, again in unison, marched forward in step with the barked orders of their captain. The crowd erupted in cheers and huzzahs. The Civil War vets paid them no mind. They marched grimly onward into the night, as if they'd been marching for a hundred years, and would march for a thousand more.

And then it became a jumble, as all the denizens of a thousand hells leaped and capered down the avenue: horned and leering demons with pitchforks; slobbering beasts out of horrid nightmares; howling werewolves in torn clothing; an entire herd of prancing centaurs; huge minotaurs stalking dangerously along swinging their massive war hammers. I saw Frankenstein's monster lumbering amidst the tumult, but there were too many vampires to count. Some were elegantly attired; some were in leather jackets and spiky punk hair, all of them with pale skin and blood red lips. There were fairies and elves, gnomes and goblins, spooks and specters and screeching ghouls clanking their chains. The crowd cheered and applauded as each clump of marchers seemed more fantastic than the one before.

Then came a huge wheeled juggernaut of a platform. Long columns of evil-looking red imps pulled the juggernaut slowly along with massive chains. Standing on the front of the juggernaut was a beefy horned demon covered with coarse hair. His cracking whip played constantly over the backs of the straining imps to keep them at their task.

And behind the whip-cracking demon was an ornate throne decorated with grinning skulls. Seated on the throne of skulls was the gigantic laughing form of His Satanic Majesty Himself, a vision straight out of "Night on Bald Mountain." A chill colder than the night settled like a pall over the crowd, and we all fell silent, the joyful cries of appreciation and applause fading away. Only the cracking of the demon's whip and the horrible echoing laughter of Lucifer filled the air. Nita shivered and pressed closer to me. I tightened my arm around her as Satan's juggernaut rolled away down the avenue, successive sections of the crowd falling silent as Lucifer blanketed each block with his withering presence as He reached it.

But then came a squadron of wild-haired witches flying on their brooms, cackling and laughing hysterically. They swooped and swirled and flung out smoking balls of fire from their wands as they whirled and circled their way down the avenue. The crowd broke into renewed cheers, relieved to see the old hags dipping and swinging and laughing above them. The weird sisters squealed with delight and flung down more fireballs to burst upon the pavement below. They were the last of the nightmare phantom parade, as no more followed them as they continued down the boulevard, wheeling and dipping and flinging their fireballs as they disappeared.

As the witches faded into the night, the crowd began to disperse. Nita and I slipped into the Starbucks and ordered two vente cappuccinos. We sipped our steaming brews and shook off the chill of the evening. It seemed so much colder than it had been earlier. And we smiled at each other. Yes, we agreed, it'd been a great Samhain Night in the Steel City. Maybe the best ever.

Eric Leif Davin won Parsec's very first Short Story Contest with his story, "Twilight on Olympus." It was later published in Mike Resnick's "Galaxy's Edge." Eric took second place in a subsequent Parsec Short Story Contest with his story, "Icarus at Noon," which was also published in "Galaxy's Edge," as well as the anthology, "The Best of Galaxy's Edge, 2013-2014," and then in a special edition anthology of "Galaxy's Edge" stories distributed at the 2015 WorldCon. Baen Books then published it in their 2015 anthology, "The Year's Best Military SF and Space Opera." Baen Books also published his story, "Avenging Angel," in the Jerry Pournelle-edited "Far Frontiers" and then in their alternative history anthology, "The Fantastic Civil War." His debut historical-horror novel, "The Desperate and the Dead," is available from Damnation Books via Amazon and Barnes & Noble. "Samhain Night" will be a chapter in a novel Eric is currently writing. Damnation Books will publish a sequel, "The Scarlet Queen," in early 2016.

Fall to Eden

by Susan Urbanek Linville

Rachel flipped up her welding visor, thinking she might get more oxygen out of the thin air than from the helmet's tube. A breeze cooled her cheeks. She leaned toward the gape-mouthed gargoyle crouched beneath the eaves of the cathedral's hundred-foot buttress. The harness twisted, tipping her momentarily sideways. Her stomach fluttered. A hundred feet down, construction cranes leaned from the support deck amid a makeshift assembly of walkways and temporary scaffolding. Below that, the sky was a patchwork of puffy stratus clouds.

She hadn't donned a fall suit today. That was strictly against regulation, but it freed her to work so much more quickly. Besides, the bulky suits might be great for a fifty-story high-rise—she'd seen a couple of workers bounce along the street, and walk away unscathed—but Saint Paul The Risen Christ Cathedral wasn't a typical building. A testament to man's elevation to the first level of heaven, the apse cantilevered out from the city in defiance of gravity. A fall from here meant a four mile descent. She couldn't imagine surviving that, with or without a suit.

She wiped her eyes, and focused on the gargoyle. A perfect weld. Some people might wonder why she took pride in this job. The gargoyles would never even been seen by most people since they faced out from the cantilevered section of the building. But that could also be said of the solar panels and dew collection system integrated into the steepled roof and no one questioned the importance of those systems. Even the hidden parts of a grand design were significant. God sees everything, not just the things visible to men and women.

She patted the wand-like device holstered along her thigh. A year ago she had been skeptical of nano-welders—give her an MIG rig any day—but nanos had their advantages. Five pounds in a backpack was a godsend when she was dangling 20,000 feet in the air with nothing between her and Eden but clouds.

"Grajek," Munnell's voice crackled over the comm. He must have noticed she'd left her fall suit in the bin. She prepared for another lecture on safety, though they both knew it was her speed and consistency that mattered to the powers that be.

"If you don't want to count your blessings," Munnell said, "I suggest you answer me."

"I'm here," Rachel said.

"I need you in the apse," he said.

"I have two more gargoyles—"

"Hughes can finish those. I've got another job for you."

Another job? Rachel frowned. She had posted nearly enough external building work to earn her Welder First Class certification. Was Munnell trying to impede her? He insisted he treated women fairly, but Rachel wasn't the only one to notice there were only two First Class women on the work crew. With the embryo implantation scheduled for her 28th birthday, she had only six months to make good on her own promotion.

"On my way." She yanked the welding glove from her hand with her teeth, and clipped it to the harness. She grabbed the rappelling rope, unlocked the anchor carabiner, and zipped down to the construction platform. Her steel-toed boots clanged on temporary grating along the north side of the cathedral. She detached from the rope, and made her way quickly around the corner.

West of the church, blocky apartments and domed greenhouses formed a repeating pattern that stretched fifty blocks to the city's opposite edge where newer construction was taller and employed more glass than steel. Wind ruffled between scaffolding pipes, nearly drowning the whine of a crane. Rachel's gaze tracked to a complex on 47th Street that she had worked on a year ago. From the outside, Repentance House resembled any other block, but it was equipped with security bars and electro-shock to rehabilitate sinners. Thank Paul there was a place for them.

A permanent ladder led up to the winch shack that extended out from the roofline. That's where the gargoyles were stored until they were positioned and spot-welded into place.

Rachel climbed down to street level, the unattached harness dragging at her shoulders. Ironically, she felt more endangered here than she had on the buttress. A slip here and she would fall fifty feet onto a hard surface. It would certainly kill her. When she worked on the cantilevered section, it felt more as if she might let go and fall forever, never hitting the hard ground at all.

She followed the building's curve past a row of plastic crates. The largest was at least thirty foot square. It must hold the rose window that would be inserted above the altar. Other windows would depict Christ, Paul the Risen, angels, and the three levels of heaven. Rachel felt a surge of warm pride. When the cathedral was finished, it would be a spectacle to behold. When she had her children, she would tell them that she had worked on this building.

She came to a twenty-foot-tall archway leading to the transept that crossed the nave. The silver-plated doors had yet to be installed. As tiny as she felt now, she could only imagine what it would feel like when construction was complete. The doors were etched with stories of Paul's revelation, God opening the Third Heaven, and Paul taking the risen Christ into himself as the Second Coming. She paused at the threshold. Could this be the job Munnell had in mind for her? If so, he was forgiven.

"It's about time." James Munnell moved into a shaft of sunlight within the apse. His work coat flapped open, revealing stained ochre coveralls and a tool belt brimming with hand tools. His red hair was shaved short, as it should be for a chaste man. A woman appeared beside him, an oval-faced Sister bundled within a dark cloak and matching head scarf. Rachel's stomach tightened. Construction workers had been ordered to give clergy a wide berth.

Munnell indicated Rachel. "This is Grajek, Sister. She'll help you."

"Sir?" Rachel glanced down. Her coveralls didn't seem too dirty, but she hadn't removed her rappelling harness and welding pack. She was hardly dressed to meet a Sister.

"Edward-Martitia," the Sister said. Rachel was struck by the creamy texture of her skin, her delicate features and full lips. The Sister was everything big-boned Rachael was not.

"I'll leave you two to it," Munnell said. He strode away, the tools on his belt clinking.

The Sister slid her hands into the pockets of her cloak. A faint odor of sandalwood stirred. Rachel remembered a girl from school. They had never been friends, had never spoken more than a handful of words to each other, but Rachel had yearned to know her. How odd. She hadn't thought of that girl in years.

"What is your given name," the Sister said.

"Rachel," Rachel murmured.

"Pretty," the Sister said. She shifted in the light, and a halo appeared around her before dissolving into dust. This is grace, Rachel thought. I am in the Lord Paul's presence. The Sister extended one hand, palm down. Rachel knelt. The touch upon her head was as delicate as the woman.

"Thank you, Sister." Rachel stood, not meeting her eyes.

"Mr. Munnell recommends you for a welding job," the Sister said. "Saint

Paul's is to host the first pipe organ ever built in First Heaven, and I am charged with overseeing the installation. I need someone to weld swell chambers and the main façade. Precision is key. There will be 28,482 pipes in all."

Rachel flushed. Twenty-eight thousand? This could take a lifetime.

"Don't look so grim," the Sister said. "The pipes are pre-assembled. You'll only have to weld the structure that houses them. The swell pipes will be installed inside metal boxes fitted with louvers to either side of the altar, which will be there." She indicated the floor beneath the largest window opening. Rachel imagined an immense platform, white steps leading up, organ pipes ranked to either side.

She nodded. "Of course, Sister, I'll be … I mean … I'm …"

"Please call me Ed," the Sister said. "I see no need for formality, do you?" She touched the back of Rachel's hand, and something stirred in Rachel, a forgotten memory, a dream. She stifled a shudder.

The shower's warm spray poured over Rachel. Sister Edward-Martitia. Ed. A Sister's clothing was cut to present a square form—no breasts, no hips—a child of God, not mere flesh. Rachel touched her own pendulous breasts. Her whole body responded. Was the Sister's anatomy as smooth as her face?

"Rachel?" Jonathan called. "Your mother's here."

"I'll be out in a minute," Rachel said. She leaned into the flow, filled her mouth, and spat it out. Grudgingly, she turned off the spigot and drew back the curtain. Her mother stood at the bathroom mirror, inspecting chapped lips.

"You're early." Rachel wrapped a towel around her torso.

"Lamb stew's in the oven," her mother said. "Your sister has to leave early. Joshua has a sports tournament."

"Soccer," Rachel said.

"Sports!" her mother huffed. "All this rushing. What is happening to this heaven? Friday evening is the Feast before Sabbath fast. A Feast is four hours. Minimum." She touched up her lips with gloss. Rachel thought of Ed's unvarnished mouth. Had the Sister ever worn makeup?

"All that running will make Joshua hungry," her mother said. "A hungry boy should not fast." She turned to Rachel. "They should do this soccer thing before dinner."

Rachel held her tongue. There was no reason to explain it again. Her mother refused to understand that feasts and fasts were unnecessary for Joshua's generation. The first conceived without fornication, they would soon be bound for Second Heaven. What mattered for them was physical strength and mental endurance. Space travel would not be easy.

Rachel's mother returned her attention to the mirror. "I spent all morning cooking,"

Rachel touched her shoulder. "Jonathan loves your lamb stew. I'm sure he'll eat several helpings."

A grin interrupted her mother's stony expression. "Tell him I will be insulted if his pants still fit tomorrow."

"Sure, Mom." Rachel squeezed around her to the bedroom. The setting sun cast red fingers across matching twin beds. She dressed in a loose shift, and scooped up a pair of soiled coveralls from the floor. Jonathan had missed the hamper again. Men. A pungent odor of fresh dirt and sweat reminded her of the day she had met him. She was welding overhead beams on a greenhouse. He was managing a harvesting crew. She had found him attractive, but it was his initiative that sparked the romance. At twenty-five, she hadn't had any interest in marriage despite her mother's best efforts, but Jonathan pursued her with such determination that when he asked for her hand, she couldn't say no.

Sister Ed was married to God. What would it be like to have a husband who took no notice, except in some ethereal way?

A ruckus drew Rachel's attention to the living area. The door slid open, and Delia's family burst into the apartment, the three kids bouncing like gas molecules from a nozzle. Joshua held a soccer ball under one sturdy arm. Katherine sang a tune out of key. Margaret, the youngest of the three, shot past Rachel to the bathroom. Her flowered dress barely covered her knees.

Rachel steeled herself, and joined the others. David gave her a curt nod before he and Jonathan removed themselves to the solarium, along with Jonathan's evening bottle of wine. Delia unpacked loaves of rye bread from a canvas shopping bag.

Margaret reappeared, dragging her grandmother by the hand, and chattering like a jackhammer. They went to the kitchen without a greeting or even a nod of recognition from Rachel's mother.

"I take it Mom's in a mood," Delia said.

"You know how she is," Rachel said. "Tradition is important to her."

"Well, it's our future that matters," Delia said. She glanced through the doorway to the kitchen where an animated Margaret was describing her latest important issue. "Thank Paul she has grandchildren to distract her. When are you and Jonathan going to contribute to the cause?"

"We've scheduled the first implantation for August," Rachel said. They had a dozen pristine eggs in cold storage, and Jonathan stood ready to fertilize at a moment's notice. She recalled the goofy smile on his face when he said that.

"Nothing like waiting until the last minute," Delia said. "You do understand that implantation doesn't always take."

"I know that," Rachel snapped. "We have two years."

"What about playmates?" Delia said. "You'll want a companion for your child, believe me." She glanced at Joshua and Margaret standing impatiently by the solarium.

"I wanted to wait until after my promotion," Rachel said.

Delia shook her head. "It's one thing to be devoted to your work, Rachel, but you should remember that a woman's primary function to bear and raise children."

"Heaven does not construct itself," Rachel quoted from the New Covenant. Delia watched her, a rye loaf clutched in one hand like a bludgeon.

Rachel sighed. They had had this argument too many times. "The past is done," she said. "Like you said, it's the future that matters. Perfect welds and perfect children will be my legacy."

Delia passed the loaf to Rachel. "Well, here goes nothing." She carried the remaining loaves to the kitchen.

Rachel stared after her, thinking of babies and spaceships, and Sister Ed's gentle touch. She ought to be upset that the pipe organ project would delay her exterior work, but she wasn't.

Three weeks later, the façade was installed and Rachel began work on the swell chambers. If she understood their purpose correctly, the louvers at the front could be opened and closed to adjust the volume. In the course of their labors, Sister Ed had provided a trove of assorted facts about the musical machine, including the importance of the pipe's positioning. She worried about the reverberation period in the cathedral. There needed to be an echo, but not too much. Six seconds was ideal. Rachel admired her passion. Ed was like a pregnant woman anxious over the birth of her child.

"People think they know what organ music is," Ed said, "but they only know synthesized sound. Even simple hymns like Holy God We Praise Thy Name and Holy Holy Holy, Lord God Almighty will roll through this cathedral like thunder. The colors, the harmonics, the swell. Nothing like it has been heard since before the plagues."

Rachel found herself nodding. "I'm afraid I don't know much about music." That didn't stop her from hanging on the Sister's every word. At the end of each day, the last thing she wanted was to go home to Jonathan.

"I'm starving," Ed said. "Let's go out for lunch." The rest of the installation crew had already left the apse.

"I don't know," Rachel said. Normally, they ate in the work trailer. Mrs. Barkley provided soup, barley bread and plenty of coffee at noon on the dot. If you went away hungry, she said, it wasn't her fault. "I'm not dressed to go to a restaurant."

Ed laughed. "And I am?" She indicated her work clothes. If anything she was filthier than Rachel. "Don't worry. It's not a restaurant I have in mind, and we can clean up on the way."

"I guess so," Rachel said. But that was a lie. There was no guesswork in her heart. She wanted nothing more than to accompany Ed, this wonderful, glowing person with whom she shared an epic quest, to lunch. She glanced at the swell tubes framing the huge window like the bones of a great hand beginning to take on flesh. She felt alive with the façade towering over her like Paul's shadow. It had been designed and built, not by Clergy, but men and women like Rachel, engineers and metallurgists, metal-crafters and coatings specialists. Welders. How could sinners have devised such a majestic thing as a tracker organ?

"It's so beautiful," she said.

"It is," Ed said. "Almost as beautiful as you."

Stunned, Rachel could only watch Ed stroll toward the open archway. Not even Jonathan had called her beautiful. He adored her eyes, her smile, the curve of her hip, but beautiful? What did you mean by that? she wanted to shout.

"Are you coming?" Ed said. She stood at the exit, framed in light from the noonday sky.

"Yes," Rachel said. She hurried down the carpeted aisle.

They took a walkway to the El station, where a worker was inspecting an array of Paul's Eyes from an overhead beam. Several of the devices were operational, brown irises constantly scanning the station for sinners. It was comforting to know that someone was watching over the flock.

They continued to the parking area beyond the station, where rows of vehicles waited impassively. Ed touched a black van trimmed in gold leaf. A door folded open. Rachel paused. She had never been inside an apostolic transport.

"Are you sure this is okay?" she said.

"Of course," Ed said. "You're with me."

Rachel took a deep breath and stepped up. The van's interior was as lush as she had imagined, with six padded recliners, and a small refrigerator.

"The lavatory is in the rear," Ed said.

They took turns freshening up while the vehicle maneuvered. Mount Ararat's cone-shaped mass flashed in and out of view in the gaps between support girders below street level.

"It's quite a sight, isn't it?" Ed said.

Rachel glanced up. "Yes," she said, caught by the Sister's smile. Ed had let her hair down. Even uncombed, Rachel found the long plaits attractive.

"Before committing ourselves to God," Ed said, "Sisters and Brothers pledge to remain as pure as Eve and Adam before they were tempted. We descend the ten-thousand steps to Eden."

"You've been down there?"

Ed nodded. "We were not permitted to touch anything. High-voltage fencing made sure of that, but there's a viewing platform just above the tree canopy. The thing I remember most is the smell. I expected a greenhouse, but…I can't explain it properly. The air is heavy with moisture, and the sweet, floral odors blend in your nose like nothing we have up here in First Heaven. Sometimes I dream I'm down there walking beneath the trees."

"I dream of space," Rachel said. "I go to the top of our apartment building and try to see the Heaven Ship."

Ed nodded. "I lived at the station for a year."

"You did?" Rachel thought of the of the space elevator's constant hum, those tiny cars bringing metal ores down from Little Moon, and carrying manufactured parts up to the station.

"I was an aide to Deacon Hallow," Ed said. "The station Chaplin. I'll probably be chosen for the Heaven Ship, but I'd rather not go."

"Why not?" Rachel said. "I would go in a heartbeat." *If I had not fallen into temptation with Jonathan. Second Heaven was only for the unstained.*

Ed gazed through the window. "First Heaven," she said. "Our salvation and our prison. It seems no matter how we try, we are subject to envy."

They passed the old cathedral, built nearly a hundred years earlier to celebrate the city's ascension to 20,000 feet. The building had always seemed so large to Rachel, but the new cathedral could hold five of the old one. Beside it sat the Golden Dome of the Holy of Holies. Only deacons were allowed inside the Tabernacle, and only the Bishop could go beyond the Second Veil to witness the Ark of the Covenant and the other holy relics.

The van drove around the building to the abbey, a structure almost as massive as the Dome. A steel façade gave the building the appearance of an open scroll bearing the words: For he looked for a city which hath foundations, whose builder and maker is God.

They parked beneath an overhang. Ed bound her hair with a scarf, and exited the van. Rachel felt self-conscious following her through the abbey's immaculate white corridors in her work clothes. She wished she had brought a scarf. At least her hair was shorn close to the scalp.

"We're late for scheduled lunch," Ed said, "but I'm sure we'll find something." They passed through a cafeteria large enough to seat a hundred. Each metal chair was neatly aligned, every table scrubbed to a gleam. In the adjoining kitchen, a Sister in a white apron glanced up from a sink of soapy water. "Leftover sandwiches in the refrigerator," she said.

Ed bowed her head marginally. "Thank you, Jacob Margaret." Rachel tried to follow her example, but felt awkward.

Ed loaded sandwiches and apple wedges onto two plates and placed them on a tray.

"Make sure you take a piece of Sister Joseph's pie," the Sister at the sink said.

"I never say no to pie," Rachel said.

The Sister chuckled. "That's as good a mantra as I've heard in a while."

Ed added a pastry wrapped in clear plastic to the tray. "Let's go outside," she said. "I'll show you the gardens where we grow vegetables and fruit for ourselves and the needy."

"I'd like that," Rachel said.

They rode escalators to the top floor, and climbed a set of steps to the rooftop. An array of greenhouses welcomed them, sunlight reflecting from glass in a thousand directions. Rachel followed Ed through a sliding door. Plants loaded with green and yellow beans bordered a walkway. Moist heat wrapped around them.

To the right of the entrance, a workbench held flowerpots precisely arranged by size. Ed pulled a stool from under the bench. "The houses are a little cramped, but I love the smell of the dirt and the greenery. I hope you don't mind."

"Not at all," Rachel said. She sat on a second stool. "After working all day on something as grand as the organ, it's nice to feel cozy." Their knees brushed.

Ed distributed food. "Looks like feta and tomatoes in the sandwiches."

"That's fine." Rachel said.

"I'd rather have chicken," Ed said. "I suppose that speaks of the corruption within me."

"Are you saying that we should not appreciate food?" Rachel said. Mom would be devastated.

"Not at all," Ed said. "Only that I should not covet something that is not on my plate. Shall we give thanks?"

"Yes," Rachel said. She lowered her gaze. Ed took her hand. A tingle shot through her. Corruption, she thought. She glanced at a Paul's Eye observing them from the greenhouse rafter. This usually made her feel at ease. Now, her stomach churned. She was trapped, the atmosphere clinging-hot.

"Let's take a walk," Ed said.

Rachel abandoned her sandwich. Outside, the air was deliciously cool. Steel fencing ran along the building's border, but the view was impressive all the same. Clouds billowed in the distance, high enough to bring rain to the city.

Ed leaned against a crossbeam. "I understand your feeling out of place, Rachel. I've been living in the abbey ten years and I still feel unbefitting. I've felt this way my entire life. Sometimes I wonder if I should have been born before the plague years. Maybe if I had lived on the surface ..."

"You don't mean that," Rachel said. "It was an awful time."

"So we've been taught," Ed said, "but when I was researching the archives for pipe organs, schematics were not the only thing I discovered."

"What do you mean?" Rachel said.

"Music," Ed whispered. "Deacons would have you believe the sinners were obsessed with fornication and greed, but that's not the case, at least not the entire case. They created more music than I could listen to in a lifetime. Songs of life and songs of love."

"The Paulines were chosen to ascend," Rachel said. "They were spared when God destroyed the others."

"They survived," Ed said. "Whether they were chosen remains to be seen."

"You don't mean that," Rachel said. "You can't say that. You're a Sister in

Paul's church, for God's sake."

"Come," Ed said. "I want to show you something."

Emotions swirled through Rachel, light and dark, and light again. It was blasphemy, what Ed suggested. Wasn't it? Wouldn't a Sister know that better than a welder? A circular white structure with a domed roof stood at the northernmost end of the building.

"I think you'll like this," Ed said. She inserted a passkey into a slot beside the door. A latch clicked. The door slid open.

Everything was dark at first, but as Rachel's eyes adjusted, she saw a silver cylinder mounted on a contraption with gears and motors. Ed pressed a button beside the door. A slit opened in the dome.

"Telescope?" Rachel had had a small one as a child.

"We don't use it often," Ed said. "Some of the Sisters like to look at the moon. Now, let's see." She touched a button, and a control panel lit. "There we go."

The telescope rotated slowly. Rachel stepped back.

"One moment," Ed said. "There are some preset coordinates here." She leaned down. "There it is." She motioned Rachel to approach. "Take a look."

Rachel closed one eye and pressed the other to the eyepiece. Ed's hand rested on the small of her back.

"Do you see it?" Ed said. Her breath was warm on Rachel's ear.

The Heaven Ship. Rachel had imagined an apartment building, metallic and square. The device that came into focus was cylindrical with arms jutting out to support smaller cylinders. One end of the main body was conical, the other attached to a platform connecting it to the station on Little Moon. She could almost make out construction vehicles traveling between the two bodies.

"It's wonderful," she said.

"When finished, it will hold ten thousand people," Ed said. Her hand edged upward. Rachel's heart raced. Ten thousand was almost half the city population.

"It would be so exciting to go," she said.

"If I could," Ed said, "I would give you my spot." She squeezed Rachel's shoulder, the pressure firm and gentle at the same time. Hairs stood up along Rachel's neck. She looked up. Ed's body radiated warmth, just inches away. She smelled faintly of sandalwood. Rachel trembled. Her legs felt like putty.

Ed leaned close. "There are no Paul's Eyes here." Rachel glanced frantically around the room. She tried to pull back, but couldn't. The Sister's lips touched her cheek. Rachel closed her eyes. She found her head turning, her mouth pushing onto Ed's. A tiny moan escaped her. She wrapped her arms around Ed's waist, and let her hands glide over the Sister's round hips. Ed cupped Rachel's breast.

Rachel's thoughts clamped down. God gave them up to uncleanness through the lusts of their own hearts, to dishonor their own bodies. "We can't," she said. "I can't."

Ed pulled back, cheeks flushed. "I'm sorry, Rachel. I didn't mean to offend you. I've been resisting this temptation for weeks."

You have? "No," Rachel said. "I..." She fought her confusion. This was sin. Stain. She should drop to her knees and pray for forgiveness. "I'm married."

"As it should be," Ed said.

Rachel stood before her husband, naked as a newborn. He hugged himself as if his clothes would jump from his body if he let go. She couldn't identify the emotions twisting his expressive face. Surprise ... delight ... Terror?

"But ... we have an implantation scheduled in five months," he said.

"I know," Rachel said. She slid her arms around his waist. His body was thick and angular. She tried to forget Ed's soft curves, her kiss. It was a mistake. She'd been caught up in the moment.

"You want to be a Welder First Class," Jonathan said. "We want our children to go to Second Heaven. What happened to that, Rachel?" He tried to nudge her away, but she held tight. His arousal was obvious. She rested her cheek on his muscular chest. This is what should attract her, the male form. Did Eve not come from Adam's rib? She should desire his hardness, his protection.

"It's been three years," he said. "Why now? Why all of a sudden?"

"I need you, Jonathan." She squeezed his buttocks. His heart beat rapidly against her ear. His breath quickened.

"You're certain?" he said. "No regrets?"

"Yes," Rachel said. The chances of pregnancy were small. Her promotion would be soon. Then they would have an embryo implanted, a sinless child.

Jonathan's arms went around her. Her body responded. She focused on his touch. This was how it was meant to be. This was what Saint Paul and God commanded. This is what I want, she told herself. But she could not forget Ed's lips, the halo momentarily surrounding her on the day they met.

When the welding was finished, Rachel found additional projects to keep her on site. She set up the pipe ranks, and sliders to open valves connecting the wind channels. She helped installers hang Paul's Eyes along the nave. Brother Allen and Brother Miller delivered the organ, and there were more connections to be made. The implantation was in less than four months, but that didn't matter. I'm helping, she told herself. This has nothing to do with Ed.

"Length determines pitch," Brother Miller said as they climbed a ladder in the swell box. He was a tall, slender man with gray hair, and at least as old as Rachel's grandparents. She was impressed with his agility.

"The fat pipes are the flutes," he said. "The skinny ones add harmonics." Rachel thought of Ed's slender fingers entwining with her own stubby digits. She learned about stop buttons and pedals, how stops could be united to make different combinations of sound. There were trumpets, oboes, clarinets. She had always thought of the pipe organ as a fancy piano, but it was really an orchestra.

Once the final connections were made, the brothers began to tune. Brother Allen played individual notes while Brother Miller adjusted the corresponding pipe, inserting a cone-like device into its top.

"Too flat," Brother Allen called out.

"It is not." Brother Miller peered down from the mini-crane. "I should have brought Jon."

"He's as tone-deaf as meatloaf."

"He possesses the ears of an angel," Brother Miller said. "How can you even suggest such a thing?'

Rachel felt a presence, and turned to find Sister Ed standing at her side. A startled thrill went through her. She had avoided being alone with Ed since the telescope incident.

"It's late," Ed said. "We should stop for the day."

Rachel shook her head. "There's so much left to—"

"I don't want to leave things as they stand," Ed said. "It's not healthy. Please come to dinner with me, Rachel. At least coffee."

Rachel stared at her feet. She wanted to agree, but how could she trust herself?

"Pie?" Ed said.

Rachel snorted a laugh. I never say no to pie. The Sister knew her better than Jonathan.

"We'll go to a public place," Ed said. "Will that make you comfortable?" She tucked a lock of unruly hair beneath her scarf.

Rachel watched the Sister's fingers work, feeling strange, even jealous. She nodded.

☼

The El train rumbled to a stop, a sleek rounded engine followed by three passenger cars. Tremors traversed the platform. Rachel heard the deep thrum of the organ's bass pipes. Natural music. Brother Miller would have an explanation for the effect.

Doors hissed open. Rachel entered the first car. Two young men in school uniforms sat toward the back. A woman with a checkered headscarf dozed next to a window, a baby cradled in her arms. Ed joined Rachel on a narrow bench. Their shoulders touched.

"I know you feel it too," she said.

"I don't know what you're talking about," Rachel said. Of course she did. She shifted closer to the train's wall, the window, the empty platform beyond.

"Homosexuality," Ed said. "That's what they called it. Not sin. Not abomination."

"Stain," Rachel breathed. Guilt pressed at her. Why did she agree to this? God, deliver me from temptation.

Ed sighed. "I sometimes wonder if there are still people down there. There were eight billion when the plagues hit."

"In Eden?" Rachel said. "They're dead. There are no survivors."

"None we can see," Ed said. "The world is bigger than you know."

Rachel swiveled to face the Sister, defiant now. "Say what you mean."

Ed frowned gently. "Earth is divided into continents, Rachel, not a single garden. Giant cities supported millions of people each, many different societies and creeds. Some worshiped as we do, some prayed to many gods. Some worshipped no god at all."

"Sinners," Rachel said.

"People," Ed said. "People like you and me trying to live meaningful lives, lives that meant something to them."

"God is my meaning," Rachel said. "And Saint Paul. What you suggest is heresy."

"Keep your voice down," Ed said. She nodded toward a Paul's Eye at the head of the car.

"Is someone spying on us?" Rachel had never thought of the devices in that way.

"Only if we give them a reason," Ed said. She pushed Rachel's hand onto the seat between their thighs. Rachel fought her. Ed would not let go. She was so much stronger than she appeared. Their fingers intertwined. Rachel stared out the window, trying not to feel the rightness of the fit between their hands.

"It seems a strange irony," Ed said, "that I, a woman married to God and Church, would find myself in this situation. Why does God place me here, why does He give me access to the knowledge that once upon a time people were free to express their love, no matter their gender?"

"This is not love," Rachel said.

"Then what is?"

The question slapped like flesh on flesh. Rachel did not have an answer. She looked to the Paul's Eye gazing down without the slightest recognition. It was blind to them, blind to everything.

"You're not alone," Ed said. "We don't have to hate ourselves for the secrets we keep."

The train slowed. "Apostolic Avenue," a voice announced. Outside, the platform was crowded with people.

"One more stop," Ed said. "I know a café—"

"I can't do this," Rachel said. She thought of Jonathan's body pressed to hers, her Mother staring into the mirror, Delia and her children. There was a right and a wrong. If not, why would it matter whether she was chaste or stained, whether she prayed, or fasted, or had children? Did she want to live in a world where a merely arbitrary ruling kept her out of Second Heaven?

She twisted her hand from Ed's grip, lurched to her feet, and shoved past the Sister through the opening door. She couldn't breathe, couldn't think.

"Rachel!"

Rachel closed her ears and worked through a maze of shoulders. A sob pushed from her stomach. In gaps between girders, she glimpsed the forested land below, a seemingly endless green.

☼

Jonathan met her at the apartment door. He looked irritated.

"Sorry I'm late," Rachel said. "I'll have your dinner ready in—"

"It's not that," Jonathan said. He glanced over his shoulder. A man with a gleaming bald pate and pointed beard stood at the room's center. Rachel's heart skipped a beat. A Deacon? His Guardian stood stiffly behind him, face hidden by a dark visor. A gleaming silver rifle was strapped to his shoulder.

"Leave us," the Deacon said. His cheeks were plump and pink, eyes beady brown. Jonathan gave Rachel an inquiring glance. She nodded firmly, and he headed into the bedroom. Rachel noticed that he did not close the door tight.

She turned her eyes to the Deacon. "May I help you?"

"No, child, I have come to help you." He glanced at a glowing screen cupped within his palm. "Rachel Grajek."

Rachel ran her hand across her scalp. "That's me," she said with her best fake smile. "Please. Make yourself comfortable, Deacon ...?"

The Deacon strolled toward the solarium. The Guardian remained where he was.

"This concerns Sister Edward-Martitia," the Deacon said.

Of course, Rachel thought. "Yes, I know the Sister through my work at the Cathedral."

The Deacon turned, expression neutral. "Let us not play games. You have been seen conversing with Sister Edward-Martitia outside the confines of your working relationship."

"We had lunch," Rachel said. "She took me to the abbey. She showed me a telescope on the roof."

"Oh?" the Deacon said. "And why would the Sister do this?"

"Because," Rachel said. *She loves me.* "She showed me the Heaven Ship. She'd heard me speak of my interest, and ..."

"Why are you interested in the ship, Rachel Grajek? You must know that your place is not there."

"I do," Rachel said. "It's just ... my children, I want my children to go to Second Heaven. I want them to be safe."

"And you think that you are perhaps a better judge of ship design than the engineers chosen by our blessed Clergy?"

"Of course not," Rachel said. "I only worry because I'm a mother." Her cheeks warmed. "Well, I will be, someday."

The Deacon looked again at his screen. "Yes. Twins."

"Twins?" Rachel's hands pressed to her stomach.

"I took the liberty of examining your medical records on my way here," the Deacon said. "You are pregnant with twins, delivery expected in roughly nine months."

Cold water splashed through Rachel. Her guilt over the afternoon with Jonathan came flooding back. How? she thought. She had had a regular check-up two weeks ago, but the nurse had said nothing of this. Was it even possible to detect twins at such an early stage?

The Deacon looked up. His expression remained earnest, but there was a hint of smug superiority in his gaze that set Rachel on edge. "Congratulations," he said. He stroked his pointed beard. "It is unusual for implantation to result in twin embryos, but not unheard of."

"But my ... our implantation, it's not sched—"

"Oh, I see that," the Deacon said. "Obviously, you rescheduled and the clinic failed to update their records. While the Clergy values efficiency, these things sometimes happen." His smile flashed. "Humans remain imperfect, I fear." His eyebrows drew close. "That is the explanation, is it not? Any other reason would be quite unacceptable to our Lord Paul."

"Of course," Rachel stammered.

"Good," the Deacon said. "Very good indeed. I will see that this oversight is corrected. We do not want innocent children to lose their places on the Heaven Ship over a clerical error."

"Thank you, Deacon." Rachel glanced toward the bedroom. Jonathan's eyes gleamed from the cracked-open door. She longed to know what he was making of this.

The Deacon nodded. "Now, may I count on your cooperation regarding the other matter I mentioned?"

"Sister Ed?"

"Precisely. How has Sister Edward-Martitia involved you in her plotting?"

"Plotting?" Rachel said. "I don't understand."

"You do," the Deacon said. "Do not be afraid. We have no intention of indicting you." He took Rachel's hands and pressed them together, as if in prayer. "All we ask is that you repent."

Rachel went to her knees. "Yes. Yes. I repent my sins."

"And confess what transpired between you and Sister Edward-Martitia."

The Deacon leaned over her, cold like the darkness above the city. She thought of the Cathedral tower, the gargoyle, the harness sliding away from her center of gravity.

"I confess," she said. "It was a mistake. I didn't mean to kiss her back. It just happened."

The Deacon stood straight, head cocked to one side. "A kiss, you say?" He stroked his beard. "When was this? Before or after your conversation about the times before the plague?"

Rachel's stomach churned. "I'm sorry. I'm feeling sick."

"Confession is your tonic," the Deacon said, "'for, with the heart, we believe unto justice; but, with the mouth, confession is made unto salvation.' First, I need your admission that you and Sister Edward-Martitia spoke of heretical subjects on the train."

Rachel looked up. "How do you know about the train? I came straight home."

The Deacon gazed at his glowing palm. "The eyes of Paul are many. You walked eight city blocks, in a circuitous fashion. Did you not believe we would move faster?"

"I didn't even know you were watching."

"God sees all, child." The Deacon steepled his hands to his mouth. "Now, did you or did you not discuss heretical matters with Sister Edward-Martitia?"

Rachel stared forward. Her knees hurt. Jonathan's eyes pressed at her back. Ed's kiss burned her lips.

"I am a patient man," the Deacon said, "but only God's patience is truly infinite."

"Yes!" Rachel shouted. "Yes. I'm sorry. We spoke of things we should not have."

"And there was also a kiss?"

"Yes," Rachel breathed. Her stomach wrenched. She tasted bile. "Once. A mistake. A mistake."

The Deacon touched her head. "You have done well," he said. "That is all we need to prepare an indictment for Sister Edward-Martitia."

"What will happen to her?" Rachel said. And what of me? she thought. She might lie to the world, but not herself. She did love Sister Ed.

The Deacon folded his palm pad into a pocket in his dark robe. "She will be detained, tried, convicted, and punished according to her sins."

"What does that mean?" Rachel said. "Will she go to Repentance House? Will I be able to visit her?"

"If you are wise," the Deacon said, "you will cut Sister Edward-Martitia from your life as one might cut a cancer from the body. The devil has had his way with her."

"Surely she can be saved," Rachel said. "Saint Paul spoke of our salvation as a gift from God, I know he did."

"Gifts can be abandoned," the Deacon said. "Or squandered. What the Sister did to you was a mortal sin. I recommend you remember that, should the urge come upon you to inflict a taint upon another." He motioned his Guardian to open the door, and exited briskly.

"They're going to kill her." The words were on Rachel's lips before she even thought them. "They're going to kill her," she said more loudly, then she was shouting. "Jonathan, they're going to kill her!"

Arms slid around her. "I'm here, Rachel."

She turned. "It's my fault."

"It's God's will," Jonathan said. "Do you truly love ... a woman?"

Rachel searched his eyes for a way out. There was none. She nodded.

"I should have known," he said. "I must seem like such a fool."

"Why?" Rachel said. "How could you know? I didn't even know."

He smiled sadly. "When I kiss you, you pull away."

"I'm sorry," Rachel said. She pressed her check to his chest. "It's complicated. I don't expect you to understand."

Jonathan nudged her away. "I don't care if you feel lust for this woman—well, I do, but it doesn't matter—but I can't comprehend how a woman—how you can risk throwing away everything for this sin ... this ..."

"Homosexuality," Rachel said. She forced her eyes to meet his. "It's not a sin, Jonathan, at least it wasn't before the Paulists took over."

"We're Paulists," Jonathan said. "We're the survivors, not them."

"I can't let her die because of me," Rachel said. "I have to warn her, I have to go to her."

"She hasn't even been indicted," Jonathan said. "You heard the Deacon. They're building a case. Stay with me. We can figure this out."

"I can't," Rachel said. She surged forward and kissed him hard on the lips, then turned and ran for the door before she could change her mind.

"I'll stop you," Jonathan shouted after her.

Rachel boarded the first train heading downtown. It was a local with many stops, but she didn't dare wait for an express, not with Jonathan's threat still banging in her ears. Even as the El pulled out of the station, she watched the platform for him. He did not appear, and she was finally able to relax. She would find Ed at the Abbey and they would hide in the city until the Clergy lost interest. Even as she thought this, she knew it would not work. The Clergy had Eyes, informants, resources. The entire city belonged to them. All Rachel had was her wits. And yet, they had eaten lunch unobserved in the telescope room. The Deacon had not seen their kiss. There must be other such places in the city, maybe a network of them.

She glanced at the Paul's Eye at the end of the car, then tucked her chin into her chest and focused on the gold band on her finger, the symbol that she had cleaved unto Jonathan. Her chest went tight. Jonathan was a good and gentle man. Any woman would be happy to have him. He should not have to suffer for her sin.

The El slowed to a stop at Northtown Station, surrounded by blocky high-rise apartments for workers manning forges a thousand feet below. At night, this part of the city glowed orange like hell's furnace. She should get off here, take the next train back. But how could she abandon Sister Ed? How could Jonathan ask her to be responsible for that? Maybe she didn't know him at all.

People got off, people got on. The train started again. She listened to the steady thrum of the tracks. Rumpa-rumpa-rumpa. Outside, lighted windows spoke of lives being lived. One extinguished as she watched. Bedtime? She thought of children on their knees, praying for dads and moms, siblings, uncles, aunts. Lord Paul, please bring us peace, lead us to the Second Heaven, and the Third. She remembered her mother's hand on her shoulder, Ed's breath in her ear. Teach us to love as we are loved. A shudder shook her.

The train's cadence changed until it felt like music to her bones, a rising tone, throaty and pure that exploded into a vibrating run of tenor notes before building again. The car banked sharply. Startled, Rachel grasped the overhead bar.

The cathedral loomed over them, dark and brooding in the night. Usually new construction was fit into the existing train grid, but the cathedral's canti-levered design had required the tracks to be recast.

The music pulled at her, until it was all she could hear.

She didn't remember exiting at St John's Station, but found herself riding an escalator to a walkway that led to the cathedral. She heard bells. No, not bells. Music. There was more air to it here, less rumbling bass. Hair rose along her neck and arms. Someone was playing the pipe organ. Sister Ed.

Rachel came to the silver-plated doors, closed for the night. A string of temporary lights dangled above, blue-white in the cathedral's shadow. One door depicted the crucifixion of Christ, the other the decapitation of Saint Paul. Rachel stood transfixed. These two great men had martyred themselves to save her soul, and yet she had chosen a sinful path.

She laid her palm on the cold metal. Deeper tones reverberated, eight repeating notes against a higher-pitched cascade of sound.

"I should go," Rachel whispered. She leaned her forehead to the doors. Music built in intensity. Eight thundering notes repeated. Rachel did not recognize the tune. Walk. Walk. Walk. Walk, it seemed to command.

She followed the wall to the construction entrance and opened the man-sized door. Warm air pushed past her. Now that the stained glass windows had been installed, the building was pressurized. She entered the apse. The music became louder, two sets of four notes, a throbbing cascade steeped in passion. Goose bumps covered Rachel's arms.

The altar stood upon a raised dais ringed by concentric circles of gray and black moon stone representing the three levels of heaven. Rachel couldn't see the organ, recessed in the floor behind the altar, but white and crimson angels were mounted to the wall beside the tallest pipes, some with swords, and some with trumpets. Saint Paul gazed down from the stained glass window while Christ looked to the heavens.

Flutes resonated. The cathedral seemed to expand with their sound. The swell boxes opened and the sound intensified. Notes repeated. Rachel knelt and folded her hands. The floor trembled beneath her. She remembered what Sister Ed had said about organs, that they were created not only to praise God, but to express the deepest needs of humankind. Saint Paul taught people to shun desire. Sins of the flesh.

The music rose in pitch and volume. Finale swelled through the cathedral, a mountain of sound and tone.

And then it was gone like a fast moving storm.

Rachel wiped tears from her eyes. She climbed to her feet and circled the altar. Sister Ed sat at the organ in her work clothes, long dark hair flowing past her shoulders. She swiveled on the bench.

"Rachel? Why are—?"

"I came to warn you," Rachel said. "The Clergy ... they're going to indict you."

"Yes, I know," Ed said. "They're coming for me in the morning. I'm to make my peace and pack my things tonight. I came here instead, to play this wondrous device before it's taken from me. I should have known the Clergy would be watching my research."

"More than that," Rachel said. "They know about us, the kiss."

Ed's expression hardened. "And how would they know that?"

"A Deacon came to our apartment," Rachel said. "He wanted to know what you told me, what we did." Her face went hot. "I confessed, Sister, it just spilled out, I don't know why."

"Because you've been conditioned for a lifetime to do just that?" Ed said. "It's all right. I've been advocating honesty to you for months. It would be hypocritical to play its victim now."

"I won't cooperate," Rachel said. "Not another word."

"There's no reason for us both to suffer," Ed said. "Tell them what they wish to know. It doesn't matter."

"You don't understand," Rachel said. "They're going to kill you. We have to get you out of here."

Ed sighed. "There's nowhere to go. Thankfully the Paul's Eyes in the apse aren't functional yet, or they would have come for me already."

"There must be somewhere," Rachel said. "The telescope room."

"We'd never get to it without being seen."

"We have to try," Rachel said. Even as she said it, she knew Sister Ed was right. There was nowhere in the city they would not been observed.

"Did you enjoy the music?" Ed said.

"It was beautiful," Rachel said. Like you, she thought.

"Carillon de Westminster by Vierne," Ed said. "That piece has not been heard for more than a hundred years. It will probably never be heard again." She closed and opened her fingers, and turned back to the keyboard. "Unless I play it again now. Would you like that, Rachel?"

"Yes," Rachel said.

"Sit with me," Ed said. She scooted down the bench to make room. Rachel sat beside her, thigh pressed to thigh, arm to arm. Sheet music stood open above the keyboard. She wished that she had learned to read music. Welding seemed such a coarse skill in Sister Ed's presence.

Ed's delicate fingers formed chords, her bare feet danced across an army of foot pedals. The apse filled with an orchestra at once competing with and reinforcing itself. Rachel released herself to the experience, the swell and swoop of the sound, vibrations deeper than she knew existed.

A noise cut through the music, a grating grind, like—

"They're coming!" Rachel said. "They're forcing the lock." She grabbed Ed's arm. "Where can we hide?"

Ed continued playing with one hand. The music lost a dimension.

"Hurry," Rachel said. "There's no time." She shoved her hip into the smaller woman. Ed slid to the end of the bench. The organ trumpeted off key and went silent. Rachel pushed frantically at Ed's back. "We have to go. Now."

"There's nowhere to go," Ed said. She looked thoughtful. "But you should leave, yes. I'll keep them occupied here. Use the construction entrance."

"That's it," Rachel nearly shouted. Her voice echoed with surprising force. "I know a place where they can't see us."

"Where?" Ed said. A snap sounded from the transect. A grating staccato filled the chamber. The great doors were opening.

"The roof," Rachel said. She stood and pulled Ed to her feet. "Come with me."

"Sister Edward-Martitia," an amplified voice boomed. "Stay where you are. We have come with the Clergy's authority. You are under arrest."

Rachel hurried through the construction entrance, dragging Ed after her. "This way," she said. They scuttled around the building's corner. The darkness was even more complete there. She felt for the ladder's steel rail. "There are no Eyes in the winch shack. We'll hide there until we can think of something more permanent."

Ed's eyes glistened, but she didn't protest. She grabbed a rung with both hands.

"Wait a second," Rachel said. "I'll be right back." She ran the few strides to a construction shed and shouldered the door open. Inside, she felt through bins until she located two welder's masks and two fall suits. With the masks clutched in one hand and a suit slung over each shoulder, she made her way back.

"Put these on," she said. The masks might make a useful disguise, and the suits would protect them should they fall from the ladder.

Fortunately, Ed was wearing pants rather than her Sister vestments. It took only a few seconds for them both to slip the loose overalls over their clothing.

Rachel donned her mask. The world dimmed even further. She watched Sister Ed's pale skin disappear behind a shield, and thought of the Guardians that were no doubt searching for them even now.

"Climb quickly," she said. "I'll catch you if you slip."

Ed started up. Rachel followed as closely as she dared. It wouldn't do to have the Sister's foot kick her visor off.

Voices sounded below. A shout, footsteps. Rachel pressed close to the building. The steel of the ladder dented her breast and hip. A light played along the building's skin. It found Ed's hand and stopped.

"Here!" someone shouted. "She's climbing."

"Go!" Rachel said. Ed continued. Too slow. Rachel moved up behind her until her torso covered Ed's lower leg. Faster, she thought. Lord Paul, please help her to climb faster.

A dart struck the ladder above Rachel's hand. She pulled back instinctively and nearly fell. Ed paused at the construction scaffolding, as if considering leaving the ladder.

"Keep going," Rachel said. The scaffolding was a dead end. It only led around part of the building, to where the gargoyles were being installed.

Ed continued up. A dart embedded in Rachel's calf. She tore it out, but not before the tranquilizer started its hot seep. Her leg began to numb. She missed a rung, caught herself, and pulled up. Hand, foot, hand. Then Ed was helping her. She had reached the roof and was leaning down.

Rachel spilled over the edge onto her back. Stars twinkled above her. So close, so out of reach. Air wheezed in and out of her lungs.

"Where now?" Ed said. "They're coming after us."

"Of course they are," Rachel said. "The shed's over there." She pointed.

"What good will that do?" Ed said.

None. Rachel thought. There must be a way out of this. Maybe they could dislodge the ladder. No, of course, not, the ladder was permanent, designed to hold a dozen men in full gear. She levered herself to her feet. She could feel the drug pounding through her veins.

"I'm sorry," Rachel said. "If it wasn't for me, you'd be playing the organ now. Jonathan must have told them."

"It was just a matter of time," Ed said. "I'm glad I got to see you again." She looked sheepish. "I know that's selfish, but I can't help it."

Rachel sneaked a look down the ladder. The Guardians were progressing slowly in their heavy gear. "I never meant to hurt you," Ed said. She squeezed Rachel's hand.

"We still have options," Rachel said. She limped past the shack to a service platform that ran along the roof's edge. Designed to allow workers to access solar panels and dew collectors, it continued as far as Rachel could see. "We'll find a ladder down on the other side of the building."

"What about your leg?" Ed said.

"Not a problem," Rachel said. But it clearly was. In a few minutes she would be totally immobilized. Still, it was worth this chance if Ed could escape. "Be careful," she said. "There's no railing." She hurried along the platform as fast as her leg would allow. Ed came behind. Rachel heard hesitation in her steps.

"I'm glad the moon isn't full," Ed said. "I can't imagine how frightening it would be to see the ground from here." This was the part of the apse that protruded out from the city.

"Don't look down," Rachel said. She made it to the far side and turned the corner. A few strides later the service platform ended.

"There's no ladder," Ed said.

Rachel wanted to cry. The roof was too steep to navigate without the platform. Bad enough her leg was losing functionality, now they had nowhere to go.

"We'll jump," she said. "The fall suits will break our momentum, and we'll blend into the night. The visors will hide us from Eyes, and—"

"There," someone shouted. Lights shown up from the ground. A line of Guardians stood in the alley.

"It was a good thought," Ed said.

"I'm not giving up," Rachel said. She started back. Maybe they could make it around before the Guardians reached the roof. The platform might extend farther on the other side of the building. If they could get to the wider street west of the cathedral, they would have a chance.

Rachel stumbled. Ed caught her from behind. Before them, the night stretched forever. The top of a gargoyle's head caught the starlight. She wondered if it was the one she had been welding.

A Guardian rounded the corner. Others crowded behind him.

"It's over," Ed said. She held Rachel's hand.

"I tried not to think about you," Rachel said. Tears dammed her eyes. "I tried to be faithful to Jonathan. I even prayed to God for forgiveness."

"Only God knows what God knows," Ed said.

A Guardian rounded the corner, visor gleaming faintly in the darkness. Rachel ran a hand across her flat belly. Two children grew inside her. Children who would be trapped in First Heaven just as she had been. They would grow up in the shadow of the world's largest cathedral, never able to ascend to Second Heaven.

She thought of green forests. The world is bigger than you know.

"Jump," she said. She couldn't see Eden, but it was there, four miles below, a seemingly endless distance that was not endless at all.

Ed looked down. "Will the suits protect us?"

Rachel wrapped her arms around Ed's waist. Her heart pounded. "I have no idea."

Susan Linville received her PhD in biology from the University of Dayton and has been writing science scripts for Indiana University's "A Moment of Science" PODcasts for several years. She has also written non-fiction books, children's fiction, newspaper and encyclopedia articles, newsletters and short fiction. She currently works part-time as Administrator for the Lawrence County Historical Society in New Castle PA, and is working on several writing projects.

You Too Shall Pass

by Russell Nichols

The father's wife was the first reflector to fall.

A 786-foot drop it was from the top of tower 101 into the ocean without end. That fateful morning, ash-colored clouds hovered like heavenly eavesdroppers. If she screamed at all, nobody heard her over the blabbering thunder. Definitely not the father. He was on the other side of his span on the Bridge to New Earth, swapping out old, corroded rivets for steel bolts, considering the name James for their newborn son. "How you know she didn't jump?" asked his firstborn, John, days after the fact.

It was an innocent question from a 7-year-old boy. A question, to be sure, that demanded an answer with no uncertain terms.

"She fell," said the father. "It was an accident."

The father was lying beside his two sons. On the floor of their unit on the lower deck of the self-anchored suspension bridge, he held his wife's gold wedding band with the inscription: SOS 6:3.

"But how do you know?" asked wide-eyed John.

"I just do."

"But how could she—"

"Do not worry," said the father, his voice true like wind. "Once we make it to New Earth, everything will be restored."

He was talking to himself, too. These were the words he carried to endure life on the bridge. The words that aided the grief in the eight years since. The words that inspired him to wait and see another day like today.

☼

Today is Metering Day.

This is the time when bridge residents get to move from their current span to the next one. Each span is exactly 2.1336 kilometers long with one tower rising 360 feet. Each tower has a local reflector, who climbs the spiral stairway every morning to look for a signal. A flash of light from a succeeding tower means the first steelers have completed the latest span and residents can move ahead. This staggered migration is necessary until the whole bridge is finished.

Metering Days can come any day. On average, it takes steelers seven years to build a new span. Not this most recent time. The father has lived in span 101 for over two decades. This is where he learned to be a steeler himself, met his wife, left his parents, had two sons, lost his wife. He's been ready to move on for a long time.

It's the sixth hour when the official yellow Metering Day lights start flashing. The father, suspended 421-feet over the ocean without end, wipes sweat and grime from his forehead. He puts nine corroded bolts in the leather bag attached to his tool belt then goes up the collapsible platform to the top deck. Metal carts rattle as upper deck residents emerge from upper deck houses to beat the rush. The father pulls off his tattered gloves, grips two cables with calloused hands. Takes a deep breath till his lungs fill up with salted air. As he does, he lifts his eyes to tower 101, a venerable pillar of steel shrouded by morning fog.

"I have to go," his wife had said before she went up that tower for the last time.

The father felt guilty in the beginning. Blamed himself for letting her go up that day. She had just given birth the month before. The sun wasn't showing. Without light, reflectors can't send signals. His wife had no reason to be up there that day. Absolutely none. But she was fixed in her ways—

A knock on his hardhat snatches the father from his trance.

"See you on the other side," says a fellow steeler, racing down the ramp to go pack up.

"Not if you lose your sight!" the father calls back in jest.

It's a classic joke, old as the bridge itself. In order to move to the next span, bridge residents must go through a toll booth, where a toll-taker scans their passbooks. Then a lottery determines what each resident must give up in exchange for passage. No one ever wants to surrender anything. But anyone who refuses to honor his or her debt cannot proceed. This is the cost of living on the bridge.

The father's been through his share of Metering Days. He's known people who've had to give up dreams or jobs or privacy to move forward. When the father was four, the lottery took his little brother's slingshot. The Metering Day after that, the lottery took his mother's left breast.

"Do not worry," his mother reassured him before she died. "Once we make it to New Earth, everything will be restored."

The father's not worried about himself right now. But he is thinking about his boys. The last Metering Day was 23 years ago. Today, his two sons will be entering the toll booth for the first time.

Either boy could be at risk.

☼

The father walks down the ramp to the lower deck. Down here, residential units line the perimeter. Small garden paths connect groups of four units to a shared kitchen in the middle. Sturdy planks extend off the deck, where fishers control mechanical fishing nets.

In the orange subdivision, the father enters his unit, a microhouse with a common room for sleeping and a cleaning room for washing. In a corner, his youngest son, James, now 8, is working on Bulbhead, his half-finished robot made from rusty, recycled materials. The head is missing.

"Son, we need to go," says the father. "You gotta take that thing apart."

"Did you bring me screws? I need more screws."

The father grabs corroded bolts from his bag, holds them in his palm. "I got your bolts here, look, look. See? But you can't have them till you're packed up, all right?"

Showing no emotion, James dismantles his metallic companion. Right then, John, now 15, rushes in, greeted by the disappointment etched into the father's face.

"What?" says John, shrugging off his guilt. "I couldn't leave without saying goodbye to Imani."

"For crying out loud, you'll see her once we pass over," says the father.

"How do you know?" says John, kneeling down to stuff clothes into an empty box.

James mutters to himself, "How do you know? How do you know?"

The father rubs his forehead, takes a breath to calm his weighted nerves.

"Listen," he says, using his hands for emphasis, "when I say be here by a certain time, you need to be here, understand?"

"Yeah, whatever," says John.

"Don't you 'whatever' me, boy. Unless you want to get left behind."

John looks up with pleading eyes. "No, no—okay, I'll be where you tell me."

The father stares at him, unconvinced.

John goes on. "I'm for real. Just don't leave me. You know I've been waiting all my life for this. I'm ready—I'll do whatever you say."

The father walks to the corner, where James is putting scattered bolts in a bag. The father brings over an empty box labeled FRAGILE for James to pack the aluminum chassis, pliers and all the wires that will ultimately make Bulbhead light up.

"All right, you two," says the father, "let's get a move on. I'd like to avoid getting caught in the crowd."

It takes them no time to pack their cart. By the eighth hour, the father and sons have left their lower deck unit and moved up the ramp. But not in time to get ahead of the gridlock. Hordes of metal carts on the top deck sound like sheets of heavy rain. On the perimeter, monitors stand guard, ready to snatch any local mooches looking to bum-rush the booths. No free passes here.

A high-pitched scream erupts from one of the booths ahead. Nobody flinches. This sound is all too common on days like this: Residents objecting to their sealed fates.

"You boys ain't nervous, are you?" says the father as they wait in line.

John snickers. "Long as I can pass, I don't care what the hell they take."

Each of them has a 1/3 chance of losing something. Bridge mandates allow families to surrender only one item—as determined by lottery—for up to three persons. For this reason, the idea of a marriage based on love is becoming old-fashioned. These days, more and more bridge residents get married and procreate primarily to offset potential losses at the toll booth.

"Is my mother on the other side?" asks James, staring at the row of red stations ahead.

John sucks his teeth. "Mother's long gone, you idiot."

"Do not call your brother an idiot," says the father, glancing back to tower 101. "No, your mother's not in the next span, James. We've got a ways to go before we see her again."

James starts to fidget. "Can I meet my mother now? I want to meet my mother."

The father puts his hand on James's head to sedate him. "Hey, hey son ... hey, did you know this bridge is alive?"

James stops fidgeting, looks down at the road. "What do you mean alive?"

"Well, the original design was a steel grid filled with concrete, right?" says the father. "But that was bad because when it hardened, it cracked."

James frowns. "Cracked? Like how Old Earth cracked?"

"Exactly, like that. So the first engineers started over with a new steel orthopedic deck."

"Or-tho-pe-dic," James says to himself as he moves forward in line. "Or-tho-pedic."

"Steel costs more, but takes longer to corrode, you see. But up ahead, two spans from here, engineers created an intelligent steel that can heal itself. As in fix its own corroded and damaged parts."

John smirks. "Looks like you're about to be obsolete then, huh?"

The father ignores him. He knows most bridge residents couldn't care less about the history. Upper deckers are content, long as they've got a good ocean view. And lower deckers are too busy worrying about how not to get left behind.

The father continues with James. "So when I say the bridge is alive, that's all I'm saying."

"I want to make Bulbhead alive," says James. "Can you get me that steel? I want that steel."

"We'll see what happens," says the father as he guides them toward the toll booth.

The father and sons approach the booth window. He hands his passbook to the toll-taker. The toll-taker scans the passbook. And waits. In that torturous moment of suspense, seconds take hours.

"What's taking so long?" asks John, not sure what to do with his hands.

The father says nothing. He holds his sons close, taking deep breaths to slow his own pulse.

Finally, a lottery ticket pops out the register. The toll-taker reads the decision.

"You sir," says the toll-taker to the father, "must surrender your peace of mind."

The father exhales as he grips his sons' shoulders. Then chuckles.

The toll-taker says, "This is only temporary—"

"Not to worry," he says, nodding. "That, I can do."

And it is done. The father's hands are still shaking as he accepts his passbook with the new stamp, grips the handle of the metal cart and leads his spared sons onward to span 102.

☼

Down the ramp, on the lower deck, the father and sons reach their new unit. Another microhouse, this time in the yellow subdivision. He parks the cart in the designated space.

"Here we are," says the father, opening the door.

Same cramped space as before. One sleeping room, one cleaning room. James carries his bag of bolts to a corner, staking claim. John looks around the place, visibly let down.

"What the hell?" he says, throwing up his hands. "It's the exact same as the old one."

"Not exactly," says the father, scratching his stubbly chin.

Then he goes to take down the full-length mirror next to the door.

John says, "What are you doing?"

"The mirror," says the father. "It's supposed to be on the far wall, remember?"

John objects. "No, no, hold on. Leave that be. I like it where it is."

"That's not where it was."

"We're in a new place."

"True, I understand that," says the father. "But I like to see myself coming in, not going out."

"Is that what you like or what *she* liked?"

In the corner, James dumps the bolts onto the floor. Then frowns.

"There's a screw missing," he says.

To John, the father says, "Why don't you go unload the cart if you want to help so bad."

John doesn't move.

"There's a screw missing," says James.

"James, all the bolts should be there," says the father. "We triple-checked, remember?"

"There were one-thousand, three-hundred and ninety-nine screws here, but now there are only one-thousand, three-hundred and ninety-eight. You lost one. We have to go back. I have to go ..."

John sulks out, shaking his head. James starts rocking back and forth, beside himself.

"Listen, son," says the father. "Hey! Look at me. I'll get you a bolt tomorrow, all right?"

James nods. "All right."

John enters, hauling the FRAGILE box. He sets it down. James goes over, drags the box to his corner to unload the other materials.

John says, "Pop, can I ask you something?"

"Feel free," says the father as he carries the mirror to the far wall.

"You're so quick to help James with—with anything really. But then, when I ask for one simple thing, you act like the bridge is collapsing."

"I didn't hear a question," says the father.

"You think moving a mirror's gonna bring her back, huh? So what, she's gonna magically appear one day? Just poof and she's there in the doorway, is that it?" John sighs. "Check, all I'm saying is we're gonna be here for God knows how long, so how about we change it up."

"I hear you," says the father, "and once you're an official member and you've gone off to get married and make babies, you can decorate your space however you well please."

John says nothing. The father hangs the mirror facing the door, then sets his wife's wedding ring on top of the frame.

"This here ain't got nothing to do with your mother. I'm doing it this way because this is the way it is. Is that straight?"

The father steps back to check the alignment.

"Straight," says John, shaking his head while walking out to finish unloading.

The father stares at his reflection, wondering if the mirror will hold up.

Three years later, John shakes the father awake.

"I'm going to apply for membership today," says John.

The dawn hasn't broke yet. Curled up on his pallet, James is still asleep. The father barely moves, worn out from back to back maintenance shifts. He can't remember his last decent rest. And his son's words make no sense until the father realizes that today is John's 18th birthday.

For an 18-year-old bridge child, applying for membership is a rite-of-passage. This means he or she can choose a mate, reserve a unit, start a family, get their very own passbook. A member can also sign up for a special assignment. In contrast to subordinate trades such as fishing, planting and steeling, special assignments represent high-level professions: reflecting, engineering, monitoring, toll-taking.

Of course, most young, new members dream to be toll-takers. No one is exempt from the lottery, but these newbies believe working the booths will give them the secret to its randomness or at least some kind of tax advantage. A classic case of youthful ignorance. And because toll-takers work only on Metering Days, they must pick up a secondary job or risk getting left behind, declared obsolete by the monitors for not pulling their weight.

The father is wide awake now. He gets up with a proud face on, reaches out to hug John.

"Come here, birthday boy," says the father, throwing pretend jabs, "or, excuse me, birthday man."

John looks uneasy, pulls away. "You'll wake James up."

"I feel like waking the whole span up," says the father, pausing to admire the man he raised. "My son. My word. My son's gonna be an engineer."

"Uh-huh," says John, avoiding eye contact.

"You going out to get the forms?" says the father. "Let me go with you."

John holds up his hand. "No, no, I'm—it's all right, pop, I'm just—I want to do this, you know, by myself is all. My first act of independence, you check what I'm saying?"

The father nods, but he senses something not right. "Can we celebrate at least? Son, this is a big step. How about this weekend, huh?"

John relents. "Okay, but keep it lowkey," he says, opening the front door.

The father frowns. "Wait, why are you going so early? The reflectors ain't even up yet."

But John has already gone out.

The least popular assignment is a reflector. Each span has one. It's the most revered position, truth be told, but requires unbelievable patience. Who wants to just sit still in one place all day? But that was her dream, the father's wife. Ever since she was little, all she wanted was to be a reflector.

Every morning, she woke at dawn and climbed the tower. Up there, she sat between the two steel saddles, behind a big mirror and waited. She'd wait there seven hours for a signal. That flash of light passed from reflector to reflector. The cue to move forward.

The father despised the job with a passion. "What if you fall?" he would always say to her. He implored her to transfer to a different assignment, something safer. Like engineering. Or monitoring. His wife refused to bend, leaving him behind with a broken heart that couldn't heal itself. But once he reaches New Earth, he will reunite with her, fully restored, as promised.

The next hazy morning, the local reflector came down from the tower saying he saw the light.

All across span 102, instant cheers of joy quickly gave way to seeds of doubt. How was this possible? Three years? No way could the first steelers finish a new span that fast, could they?

Given the overcast, the reflector requested that Metering Day be postponed so he could verify the signal tomorrow. With that decision looming, the father decided to celebrate his son's soon-to-be membership with a small banquet on tonight.

At half-past the eighteenth hour, the father and sons are eating in the shared kitchen with fellow yellow subdivision residents. As they take fresh fish and bread, a restless energy hangs over the room. Everybody looks charged up. Except the father, who looks absolutely fatigued, dealing with a migraine.

At the round table, he removes the bones from James' fish.

"Bones are bad," says James. "No bones for me, thankyouverymuch."

Across from the father, John sits next to Imani, his longtime girlfriend, now fiancée, a first-year toll-taker, who also works as a bean planter.

John puts his arm around her. "So what's the deal, my little toll-taker? We moving tomorrow?"

Imani shrugs. "I don't have the foggiest idea, beloved."

John points to the custom-made steel ring on her finger. "But I only proposed 'cause I thought you had the inside track, love."

She feeds him a chunk of fish. "Oh hush. You proposed because you recognize a good catch."

John eats, but keeps up the deadpan. "I feel so ... conned," he says. "Reckon I gotta go find somebody else, then. Start a hedge family—"

He can't even finish the phrase without cracking up. He pulls Imani closer, puckers his lips all fish-like until she kisses him. A wizened little lady, who lost her voice last Metering Day, grins at the display of young infatuation. A rarer sight nowadays. But the nuzzling session gets interrupted by Tomás, a bearded teenager who lost his innocence last Metering Day.

"But you do bring up a good point though, John," he says. "I mean, not about your engagement. Congrats on that. But what if this whole bridge thing is one long con?"

John tilts his head. "How you mean?"

"I mean, like …" Tomás pauses, leans forward. "Okay, so we know for a fact that this planet broke … somehow."

"Somehow?" says Imani.

Tomás smirks, holding his hands up in defense. "Listen, I don't believe the quote unquote comet apocalypse actually happened … but whatever, that's another story."

"Here we go," says Tomás' father, a one-armed pepper planter, dropping his head in his hand.

"All speculation aside," says Tomás, "we know our ancestors started building this bridge. Presumably to get off this fractured planet, right? But who knows where we're going?"

Mute elder writes in Chinese on her portable chalkboard: 'New Earth'

"Right, okay," says Tomás, "but, check, what if New Earth is not a desti-nation, but a concept. What if it's toll booths all the way down? Or even worse, uh … how do I say this?"

"What are you trying to say?" says John.

"Well, truth be told, I think this whole thing is a setup. And the reflectors, they're all in on it. They're herding us to some black hole, so they can have what's left of Old Earth all to themselves."

Imani stares at him, blankly. "Are you unstable?"

"Do excuse my son," one-armed planter says to the father. "My boy didn't mean no disrespect to your late wife."

The father keeps eating his fish, too tired to engage the bearded conspiracy theorist.

Tomás says, "No sir, no offense intended. I'm just saying, we're always moving, moving, moving, but it don't seem like we're getting much of any-where."

"Neither is this conversation," says one-armed planter.

Tomás looks around the table for support. "John, you check what I'm say-ing, right?"

The father lifts his eyes to John. John rubs his chin, considering.

"I do wonder," he says, "if we're really headed to this New Earth, it seems like somebody up there, out in front should've seen it by now. A glimpse at least."

Mute elder writes on her chalkboard: 'cannot see New Earth until bridge finished'.

Nobody understands her brand of wisdom, but the monitors already declared her obsolete, which means she will be left behind. Knowing this, the group does not question her.

To Tomás, one-armed planter says, "Eat some bread, son. It'll help get rid of that foot-taste."

Yielding, Tomás slumps back, takes a bite of bread. Copying him, James bites his bread too. The father gets back to chewing his fish.

To break the awkward silence, Imani pinches John's cheek and says, "Guess we'll have to wait for you to tell us what you see, Mister Reflector."

John nudges her. Too late. Imani winces, realizing she overshared.

The father stops chewing his fish.

Tomás springs forward. "You're gonna be a reflector? Man, that's so rusty!"

The father puts down his fork.

"My mother was a reflector," says James. "I'm going to go to meet her."

The father takes a drink of water.

John clears his throat. "It's no big thing. I doubt I'll get the assignment."

"I don't see why not," says Tomás. "The monitors got to pick you. This is in your blood, bro …"

One-armed planter puts his hand on his boy's neck. "Son, I think it's about that time."

"… and even if they don't," continues Tomás, "I mean, maybe my opinion don't hold up because I'm not a member yet, but still, I say you got balls for signing up in the first …"

His voice trails off when he sees what mute elder has written: 'stop talking now!'

Tomás frowns, then realizes. Across the table, the father is glowering. The room turns eerily silent, held hostage by tension. The father sees no one else. Only John. His firstborn. A liar.

John cannot face his father. He stares at his empty plate.

"I made the decision I made," he says to the plate. "That was my natural right. My choice. Nobody else's. If you can't respect that, you don't respect me. Or my mother."

The father stands. He picks up his plate. He scrapes the remains of fish into the compost chute. He takes James' plate. Scrapes that one. Washes both of them.

Then the father ushers James toward the door.

On the way out, James says, "My mother was a reflector, but she's long gone, right John?"

The door closes.

Today is Metering Day.

The yellow lights started flashing at the sixth hour, which means the verification signal came through. By the ninth hour, the upper and lower decks had become a snarl of metal carts and antsy bridge residents carrying umbrellas. The sky looks just about ready to crack.

The father is standing in the lane farthest to the left. He didn't sleep a wink. John stands next to him. They do not speak

In the crowded line, James pushes the cart forward. The father looks at his secondborn. Feels like just yesterday he was 8 and they were moving to span 102. Now, here they are, approaching 103, walking up to the toll booth for another lottery.

The father knocks on the window. "So I heard this booth is giving out free passes?"

Inside, Imani smiles wide.

"Hey! I was hoping I'd see you guys," she says, accepting the father's passbook.

James points at Imani. "I remember you."

"I remember you too, big man," says Imani to James, scanning the father's passbook.

While waiting for the lottery ticket to pop out, Imani looks at John, heaviness on his face.

"Beloved," she says, "I thought you were getting your own passbook."

He groans. "I tried to expedite, but the monitors postponed all pending applications—"

"Right, of course, because of Metering Day," she says. "That makes sense."

John shrugs.

"Hey," she says. "Don't look so down. It'll be there after you pass."

Imani kisses two of her fingers, presses them against the window. John takes a breath and just as he lifts his fingers to meet hers, the lottery ticket pops out. Imani's smile suddenly fades.

"What's the verdict?" asks the father.

She tries to compose herself to read the decision, but can't hide the hurt in her eyes.

"Your oldest son …," she says, fighting back tears. "Your oldest son must surrender his sight."

"What?" says John.

"No, that can't be right," says the father.

Imani wipes a tear from her cheek.

"This is …," she starts, then stops and starts again. "This is only temporary. Once you reach New Earth, everything will be restored."

The father pinches the bridge of his nose, squeezing shut his weary eyes.

"Imani," he says, "there has to be another way to—"

The father stops when he feels a hand on his shoulder. He turns around. Sees John standing there, shaking his head.

"This is the way," he says. "I will do this."

And it is done. After that, James pushes the metal cart while the father helps guide his blind firstborn onward to span 103.

The new place looks just like the old place. Another microhouse, this time in the red subdivision. The first thing the father does is move the mirror to the far wall. He sets his wife's ring on top, as usual. James arranges his mechanic's corner, as usual. But over the next week, John really struggles to adjust to everything. He mopes in the unit all day, weighed down by a range of stress.

One late afternoon, the father guides John out to follow up on his membership application, but stops at a spot near the fishing planks. John objects adamantly. But the father tells him he needs fresh air. They stand there, on the lower deck, gripping the rust-free metal railing while the sun bows out.

"This is life, son," says the father. "It ain't the end of the world—"

John shakes his head. "I swear, if you say anything about other fish in the damn sea—"

"But that's true, whether you believe it or not."

John scoffs. "You tell me what's true. Tell me you told Imani to break up with me."

"The lottery made her give up her feelings, John, you know that."

"Not that I blame her," says John. "Only a fool would marry a blind, soon-to-be obsolete man."

The father stares down into the ocean without end. He hasn't told either son about his own struggles. Turns out, the mythical "living" steel can heal itself after all. That means on span 103 and all spans ahead, steelers have become redundant. At the father's post-pass check-up, the monitors gave him two weeks to find a new job or he will be declared obsolete. But he keeps this to himself.

"When I was your age, about 18, I was training to be a journeyman," says the father. "This was back in span 101. Before you were born. I'd just married your mother and, uh, we had a big fight over something—I can't remember what. Something trivial." The father chuckles. "I think it was over where to hang that mirror, now that I think about it. I can't remember exactly. But I came to work all stressed out and whatnot, wanting to quit. And that's when my mentor told me about loads."

"Loads?"

"He said—and I never forgot this—he said, 'every suspension bridge has its limits. But the ultimate strength and stability of a bridge depends on how well it's been built to handle certain forces. Structural engineers call these forces loads.' Then he went on to break down the three main types: the dead load, live load and dynamic load. See, the dead load is the weight of the bridge itself. The live load is the weight of traffic moving over the bridge. And the dynamic load is any outside forces, you know, like wind and other extreme weather, you follow me?"

"Check."

"Which one you think affects the bridge the most?"

"I don't know. Dynamic?"

"Well, you're smarter than I was," says the father. "Right, dynamic loads are the tricky ones. They creep up with no kind of warning. Can't be measured. Can't be contained. But harsh conditions test integrity. If the structure can't go with the wind, so to speak, the bridge will shift. Or collapse."

For a moment, neither of the men speak. Over the whistling wind, they can hear the chants from fishers, the clang of the mechanical fishing nets and the churning waters way down below.

Finally, John turns to the father and says, "How the hell is that supposed to help me?"

The father takes a deep breath. "C'mon, let's go get this membership handled."

An hour later, the door to the microhouse bursts open. James, working on Bulbhead in his corner, barely even reacts as John storms inside, a man on fire.

"This is pointless!"

The father comes in after. "John, slow down. Get your footing."

John clenches his jaw as he feels around to get his bearings.

The father turns to his secondborn. "James, go get washed up for supper."

James keeps his eyes on his robot, which now looks just about complete, standing 12-inches tall with rusty pliers for arms and aluminum tubes for legs. A lightbulb head sits firmly in a socket. James tinkers with wires inside the chassis.

James mutters, "Almost finished."

John feels his way along the wall to the cleaning room.

"James, wash up now." The father goes to knock on the door. "Son, open up."

From behind the closed door, John says, "There's no point. They rejected me. Just like Imani."

James adjusts the wiring. Bulbhead's head flickers on, then off, then on. Illuminating the corner.

James' eyes grow wide at his creation. "Am I finished?"

To the closed door, the father says, "The monitors said you could re-apply …"

Suddenly, a twinkle in the light catches his eye.

There, on the ground amid the defective nuts and bolts, lies his wife's wedding ring.

The cleaning room door opens. John comes out.

"Re-apply?" he says. "Re-apply for what? I got no marriage prospects. I can't be a reflector now. And don't act like you ain't happy about that."

The father stares at the ring on the floor. "James, where'd you get that ring from?"

"It's my ring," says James, without turning around. "You don't bring me screws anymore."

"It's not your ring, James," says the father.

John rambles on. "They might as well get it over with and declare me 'functionally obsolete'."

"It's my ring," says James. "It was a gift."

John bangs his hand on a wall. "No, no—I refuse to get left behind!"

The father picks up the ring, turns to John. "John, did you say James could have this?"

"Who cares?" says John.

James mutters, "I like my ring, thankyouverymuch."

"It doesn't belong to you," says the father to James.

"It don't belong to you, neither," says John to the father.

The father says, "Excuse me?"

John says, "Did the lottery take your hearing?"

The father raises his finger. "Watch your mouth, boy."

"I got no vision, remember?" says John, then starts laughing. "That's the sad thing about this. I'm the one without sight, but you can't even see the truth right in front of your eyes."

The father tenses up, "What truth? That I spent all my days hanging off this goddamn bridge, huh? Working overtime to make sure we don't get left behind? Keeping bread in your belly, clothes on your back? That truth? Steeling is all I know. And all I do is try to support you both. I am your father."

"You're a liar!" says John. "You don't know shit about shit. All you do is lie. About New Earth and everything being restored and mom falling off that tower—"

"What'd you say to me?" says the father.

"Everybody on the whole bridge knows she jumped and it's your mother-fucking fault—"

Without warning, the father charges his firstborn. Slams him against the wall. The impact shakes the mirror from its nail. It hits the floor, but remains intact.

Through gritted teeth, the father speaks.

"Say what you will about me, but you will not disrespect your—"

John throws his fist into the father's gut. The father hunches. The wedding ring slips from his grip, pings onto the floor. James scrambles under his pallet, screaming his lungs out.

"STOP IT! STOP IT! STOP IT!"

The father heaves John across the common room.

John slides backwards, grasping air for something to hold.

Stumbling over James.

Slamming into Bulbhead in the corner.

The rusty robot topples over. Nuts and bolts shoot every which way. The lightbulb cracks and goes out as it hits the floor next to the gold wedding band.

Today is Metering Day.

It's been six years since the father last saw these flashing yellow lights. Six long, tired years. John has barely spoken since the fight. He never re-applied for membership. Pride made him stiff. It was unusual for a 23-year-old bridge child to be unmarried, jobless and living with parents. John spent his time helping James study applied science and holding his "stash of screws". James, now 17, made John a metal walking stick and worked on bringing Bulbhead to life, better and brighter than ever.

Meanwhile, the father had to pick up two new jobs—as a fisher and carrot planter—to make sure monitors didn't declare any of them obsolete. His body languished under the pressure of hard, backbreaking labor. His knee brace can't hide the limp now as he makes his way toward the toll booths.

"See you on the other side," calls out a fellow fisher with his hedge family a few lanes down.

The father just nods. James pushes the cart forward in the far right lane. The father looks ahead, sees tower 104 rising into blue sky. Not a cloud in sight. The sun beams down on the upper deck, reflecting off the stream of metal carts and shooting back up along with all the screams of suffering.

It's the twelfth hour when the father and sons reach the toll booth. The toll-taker scans the father's passbook. And waits. The father wipes sweat and grime from his forehead with his calloused hand. He looks at his sons, in awe of how much they've grown in such a short time. His wishes their mother could be there to see them. Do not worry, he reminds himself. In due time.

The lottery ticket pops out the register. The toll-taker reads the decision.

"Your youngest son—"

"No!" says the father, his hand on the window. "No, no, no. Whatever it says, the answer's no."

"Sir, please," says the toll-taker.

"Please what?! Surrender what? His ingenuity? His imagination?"

"What do I have to give up, Mister Toll-taker?" asks James, holding up the gold wedding ring.

"Your life," says the toll-taker.

The father's knees buckle. He falls to the deck.

"NO! You're not taking my boy from me!"

John steps up to the window, shielding his younger brother with his metal walking stick.

"I'll do it."

"You know that is not allowed," says the toll-taker. "I'm truly sorry for your loss."

The father is on his knees. Tears in his eyes. Hands folded.

"I beg you … don't do this."

"Sir …," says the toll-taker.

"Listen, I been working on this bridge longer—hell, longer than you been breathing, I'm betting. I paid my debt. And, and he's just a … he don't deserve—"

"This is only temporary," says the toll-taker. "Once you reach New Earth, everything will be—"

"—will be restored?!" interjects John, pounding on the window. "How do you know?! How do you know, huh? Have you been there? No, no—you don't know. You don't know shit about shit!"

His left arm weakens, flopping against the window as he breaks down. The father stands to his feet to console his firstborn. John stumbles back. But the father finds the strength to hold him up.

John surrenders, covering his distraught face. "I can't carry this …"

The father whispers into John's ear. "Remember the loads."

Then the father turns to his oblivious secondborn. James is holding the wedding ring up to his right eye, looking at the tormented people in line behind them.

The father puts his trembling hand on James' head, way higher than it used to be.

"James," he says, "Your brother and I have to go away for a little while, all right?"

"All right. Are you getting more screws? I need more screws."

"While I'm gone, you'll get everything you need."

"That's good. Screws are good."

"And when I see you again, you'll be finished with Bulbhead, right?"

James opens the father's left hand and puts the gold wedding band in his palm.

The father kisses him on his forehead. "See you on the other side, son."

After John hugs his younger brother, a monitor comes and takes James away. The toll-taker hands the father his passbook with a new stamp. The father exhales, looking onward to span 104.

But as he reaches out to John, his firstborn pulls away.

"I'm not going anywhere."

"Listen, son, trust me, I know this is not easy. It doesn't always feel good. But this is the way," says the father. "We have to keep moving."

John shakes his head.

The toll-taker says, "If you choose to stay behind, you will be removed from the family and declared obsolete. You will not be allowed to pass later, do you understand?"

John picks up his walking stick and lifts his head into the sunlight.

He takes a step backwards. "I have to go."

"Please, son!" says the father, breaking. "Don't turn back. Don't leave me. I can't lose you too. We've come too far. We're so close!"

John hands the father his walking stick.

"No we're not."

Then John turns around, feeling his way in the opposite direction. The father stands still, calling out. But his firstborn is lost in the crowd, a drop of rain in an ocean without end.

☼ ☼ ☼

Russell Nichols is a speculative fiction writer and endangered journalist. He writes about race, class and other human myths. Raised in Richmond, CA, he now lives on the road, out of a backpack with his fairytale freak of a wife (current location: India). Look for him at russellnichols.com.

The Seven Wonders of a Dying Planet

by Mary J. Daley

Ghosts populate the ruins of this city. Some are featureless, resembling nothing more than wood smoke, while others retain a somewhat ashy distinctiveness. They wander up and down the streets, enter and leave buildings, and are as numerous as the bots that still twitch and sputter about our feet.

One ghost, near the south steelworks, tilts her head and runs her hands over her curves. She's standing in five-inch stilettos and dressed in her own shadow, which only enhances the size of her breasts. It's difficult to determine if she's soliciting us, or even sees us.

The steelworks' massive doors are missing, leaving the interior gaping like a split beast. Barrel-size welding bots with torches long extinguished move slowly about the aisles. They're the ones responsible for all the metal fabrication that was done on this planet, back in the days when the mines were operational, before the land disputes and air attacks. Some of their work still graces the skyline in dirty pewter.

Between the ghosts, the bots, the steel, and our silver assayer suits everything here is unified in color. That is until Talart turns to offer Frond a wide smile and her plum lipstick changes the landscape.

"We'll visit the horses first," she says.

I look over my shoulder to a line of hills in the distance. When I turn back I catch Frond looking at me. He has noticed my calluses the evening before, and is beginning to grow suspicious, wondering where I'm sneaking off to on my rest days.

I can't quite find the words to tell him that I keep returning to Cradle 8, the last mine we assayed, hoping to pull him and the Talart from the rubble. I would have gone down again today if Frond hadn't insisted that I come into the city with them.

I have Talart almost free but Frond is buried deep. Before I tell them what has happened, I first need to ensure them that I'm taking them home. I thought I had more time but Frond is already talking about readying the ship for departure.

Maybe this pursuit of Talart's may delay things?

She has taken a great interest in the steel art here, especially the chariot horses in the plaza. She believes it's an original sculpture by the famous artist, Noa Sicab, who has graced the first colonies with several magnificent works before she went into hiding. Frond believes that Talart is slightly delusional.

Talart joined our team two years ago and although she is a qualified geologist, she's far more interested in art then assaying ore.

Her excitement, however, is contagious, and Frond, perhaps needing this distraction, keeps joining her on these forays into the city. I'm not complaining because every day we're not preparing for departure is one more day I get to avoid telling them they're dead.

☼

Frond sticks his boot out to stop a rat-size bot that is crossing the road. When it reverses slightly to change course, he sweeps it up in his gloved hand and studies it. "It looks like an old vaccine distributer," he says, before setting it down so it can continue on its way. "Do you think if a virus dies here it gets copied too?"

I freeze momentarily. Talart simply shrugs.

A translucent boy of about nine years old comes out of nowhere and squats beside the same bot. He tries several times to pick it up but fails in his attempts. He finally gives up and runs off.

"How long do you think he's been here?" Frond asks.

"I'm guessing he died during one of the raids, which would make him about eighty years dead," Talart answers. "But the mines here have been leaking ghost gas for ages, so who knows."

I find this conversation crushing. They are oblivious to their fate and it's my fault. But the moment I tell them it will change everything.

Maybe nothing could have prevented the accident that killed Talart and Frond, but we were all issued filter masks, and so what they are now could have been prevented. We stopped wearing the masks months back because the gas is harmless to living things, and we were just planning on getting our work done and going home.

My breath hitches and I cover my eyes to hide my tears.

"What's wrong, Alma?" Talart asks. She glances quickly at Frond, perhaps believing he's to blame for this. And yes, in some ways our recent breakup is combined in all this, but now it feels a hundred times more permanent. I'm not ready to give him up. I already miss him.

We reach the plaza by midafternoon. The shadowed manes of the five horses appear more hair than steel. Their hooves are slightly tarnished and the chariot they pull is pitted. Grey scrub grass lines the cracks of stone around their hooves. It's not actual grass but the sub-energy of earlier grasses.

Talart removes her gloves and brings her hands over each horse, over each flaring nostril and across the steel straps of the chest harness. She loves this sculpture. Ever since we came across it during our first trip into the city, she talks of little else. I stand in front of it for a moment. The sensation that they will run me down is so palpable I have to step aside.

"How was she able to create such perfect beasts?" Talart asks.

Frond is leaning against the chariot's wheel, shading his eyes with one hand. "It's not that difficult. The bots probably copied them from an episode of Ancient Earth."

"This is definitely not bot work. It's exquisite. It's by Sicab. I know it is. And I believe I have found yet another sculpture of hers. A slightly more portable piece to bring back with us."

"Talart, we don't have room to bring anything back with us," Frond says.

Talart looks at me wistfully, wanting me to back her on this plan. I try to smile. She almost smiles too but not quite. "As soon as Quantum Resources is able to accept our dismal findings here, they're going to auction off this entire planet to a salvage company for next to nothing. All we have to do is secure the salvage rights and we'll never have to assay another mine as long as we live. I guarantee it. Just let me show you what I've found so I can convince you." At a jog, Talart heads northeast.

"She sure is passionate. We have to give her that," he says. He watches her run until she disappears down a side street. My cheeks begin to burn. I'm breathless over the jealousy I feel.

When we catch up to her, she is standing near a six-story building that looks somewhat stable. Talart grabs Frond's hand and pulls him forward. He grunts but follows her into the building and up a stairwell that is missing sections of its inner wall. Neither looks back to include me. I follow anyway.

Two ghosts in their teens pass us on their way down. Up close, their faces are faithful to youth. One boy blinks, returning his mist-colored irises briefly to blue. The effects of this planet's gas are vast, devastating and creepy as hell.

In the living, it leaves the cells entirely after several deep breaths of cleaner air. But upon death, if even minute amounts remain in the body, it prevents the sub-energy of an organism from dispersing, trapping the shape to its original form.

Talart leads us to the fifth floor and opens the third door on her left.

We follow her into a spacious living area, where a meter long steel sailing ship sits encased in glass. Its detailing is so fine its sails appears to billow.

"How do you know this is by the same artist?" Frond barely glances at the art. Instead he plops himself down on the only chair in the room. I sit on the floor with my head against the wall.

"Maybe not the same artist but definitely the same method," Talart says. "And if I'm right this artist and the ones who studied under her produced these works during the early half of this planet's settlement. The same time period that Sicab grew tired of public scrutiny and went into hiding."

"I say it's bot work." Frond studies the creases in his gloves.

She shakes her head and runs a hand over the glass looking for a way to open it. "And this is a perfect size to have appraised."

Her hope feels ridiculous now. I sigh too loudly.

She looks over at me, her eyes still full of expression. "What can I do to convince one of you, so I can hold the majority vote here?"

As Talart bends to peer closer to the glass a tall, thin ghost runs in from the corridor at her, flailing his arms. She screams and falls backwards. Frond laughs. The ghost, who is wearing nothing but a bathrobe as grey as the rest of him, continues to move about the room. He visually stomps about with exaggerated but silent steps.

Frond is still chuckling.

"Let me help you up," he says to Talart.

She offers her hands. He grabs them, pulls her up and against him.

"You should've seen your face. He scared the living shit out of you," he says.

"Why did he do that?" She is much too close to Frond, practically talking into his cheek.

"Because you're talking about stealing his sailing ship." My tone is harsh, causing Talart to step away from Frond. I get up slowly. My lower back is still stiff from digging. It takes me a few minutes to straighten. I don't care to see any more art. I want to return to the ship.

☼

The surveying ship we've been calling home for the last year is forty meters in length. Ore samples and assaying equipment take up most of its space, making living quarters tight. Especially now that Frond and I no longer share a bed.

Frond falls back into the cockpit chair and removes his boots. He still appears natural. He is solid and real and I want to go to him, hold him, tell him how much he still means to me.

"If we leave some of the older equipment behind, we could make room for it." Talart comes in behind us and pulls off her silver hood revealing vibrant red hair.

"Leave it, Talart. Let's just concentrate on finishing up here, so we can get home." Frond says.

"Why? So we can be sent to some other crappy planet. Just one piece, Frond."

"You took plenty of footage. Shop that around." He runs his hands over his face. "I'm sorry, I don't have the patience to discuss this anymore. I'm going to bed." He moves past us and into the sleeping area, sliding the door shut.

How long he and Talart will remain solid is undetermined. The effects of this gas give a life-like presentation in the beginning stage, right down to sensation, pigment, and interaction. Over time, with the decomposition of the original cells, this all fades until only bone holds what is left of the image.

Talart waits, tapping her fingers against her thighs. It grows dark in stages until the lights along the ship's ceiling looks like an illuminated-spine. Talart unlocks her storage bin. Inside is a steel plate with an intricate, raised floral pattern around its edges. Beside it sits a steel sparrow. I go over and stand next to her as she cups the perfect bird in both hands. "Don't tell him I have these, Alma," she whispers.

"They're beautiful," I offer.

"But too small to attract much attention, and I can't simply shop the images of those horses around. The worth of her art is in its physical presence. You know what I mean. You stood in front of them. You felt them. Will you help me?"

I nod. I want so much to help both of them but I don't know how much more I can do on my own. I have begged the company to send another ship but they're hesitant. And even if I manage to free Talart, Frond is buried much deeper than she is. But I have to try.

"Talart, if you can convince Frond that I need another day to go off on my own, I'll stand with you regarding the art piece and outvote him."

She frowns. "Thank you. But I wish you weren't spending so much time alone. Frond is getting worried. If you need company, or someone to talk to, I'm here. I know you said you don't want to discuss him but I knew you guys since field school. I know how much you once meant to one another."

"I think you mean to say what we still mean to one another." It comes out sounding like a warning.

Talart nods and focuses again on the sparrow.

The next morning, I return to the mine where they lay under rock. I take the long elevator down and walk through the rubble. There is only one functional calf-high light bot in this section of the mine, and it recognizes me now. It stays close, offering just enough light to see by. Talart is partially uncovered. Her wrists are purple from where I pulled on them, thinking at one point I could simply pull her free. I resume digging, ignoring the pain in my back.

I was spared their fate only because I was lagging so far behind them on the day of the quake. I was in my head trying to dissect bits of his garbled breakup speech, still trying to determine if I could fix us somehow. The first tremor literally shook me from my thoughts, and I reached for a steel support beam. Frond and Talart reached for each other. He looked back at me, making sure I was okay, when a rock shard, the weight and size of one of those steel horses that Talart loves so much, came loose from the wall and fell, crushing them both. I knew by the impact that they were both dead even before the rest of the wall came sliding down to cover them. I managed to scramble away from the slide and back to the elevator.

Once on the surface, I sat in the buggy with my head on the wheel and waited for the rattling noise of the elevator to start up. I thought I knew what to expect because the effects of ghost gas is well documented, going as far back to the first known case here, where a mine explosion killed forty miners, all of whom returned to their bunks that very same night.

However, when Frond and Talart slid into the buggy beside me some time later, I would never have taken them for copies if I hadn't witnessed what that rock had done to them. They were fine. Not a scratch on either, and they acted like it was the end of a normal shift. So I drove them back to the ship and said nothing about what had happened. On my next rest day, I went down and began removing the rocks.

Finally, after all my attempts, I free Talart. I then begin pulling rock away from where I believe Frond is buried. But it's impossible. The rocks are massive. Even if I brought Frond down here to help, we won't get him out. And I can't bring him down here only to show him that he's here forever. I write his name in bold letters on one of the bigger rocks. I remain on my knees for some time. The bot waits for me. It appears solemn and reflective too and I'm grateful it will remain down here with Frond.

I drag Talart to the surface and into the buggy, trembling at the mere thought of Talart seeing her busted body. However, they are gone when I arrive back. It is a mixture of relief and disappointment I feel. I am quick to place her in a container bag and hide her in the ship, behind the ore samples and equipment.

I then reach for the communicator and switch it on. It's a clear night and I am able to reach Union Station and the Quantum Resources work department. I still blame them partly for not accepting our first thorough evaluation. They kept insisting on more data even though we knew this planet couldn't possibly go through another resurgence. These mines go to such unfathomable depths it's a wonder this planet hasn't split in half.

This time my request to speak to the CEO is accepted. I sigh with relief.

"I need you to send a crew here," It comes out so quick it sounds neither like a plea nor a demand, but something else entirely.

There's a pause. The CEO clears his throat. "We can't facilitate this."

"And I can't leave him here. Please. You have to."

"We are not liable. Read the contract. But we're not without compassion and will provide compensating packages to their families. And if you can return with the bodies, we'll finance the extraction of the gas, releasing their copy. It is all we can do at this end. "

"But you don't understand, Sir. They're still not even aware it happened. How do I tell them? We're preparing to leave and I was only able to rescue one. How can I part them? They're always in each other's company." As I say it, I realize how true these words are. In my distress, I've failed to notice just how much time I spent down in that mine, and how much time they've spent together.

"Alma, I can only advise you to proceed with a routine departure. They're tied somewhat to their physical bodies, which means the one who is still trapped will return to the surface after enough distance."

I end the call.

☼

The next morning I'm so stiff I have trouble sitting up. I hear laugher. It is light and is followed by a deep chuckle from Frond. I pull myself from bed and step into his sleeping compartment, finding Talart in there with him. I'm not surprised. It was fated. Frond and I have always been too much alike, too inflexible, while he and Talart look like they could achieve balance.

Talart sees me first and goes still.

Frond looks up and says, "What the hell, Alma?"

I flip them my middle finger and leave. I'm trying to be respectful, but I'm angry. I hate them both for this exclusion.

I go to the water tower that is not a tower anymore. The base has been knocked from it ages ago, leaving its wide silver container to lay diagonally across a series of elevated rocks. Inside, approximately one thousand gallons of water remains trapped. It's a pristine, totally protected swimming hole that is cavernous and dark, with just enough fluttering green fluorescence in its walls to see by. The tilt of the container makes for a dry bank along the edges of its warm, ancient water.

Frond and I had found it about six months ago. It was a godsend then. Not because our ship wasn't equipped with a proper water system, but because our relationship was failing and this quiet oasis for a time made us forget that it was.

I stand with my toes in the water and try to remember why Frond and I stopped coming here. Or when we stopped coming here. Was it after or before Talart found the horses? She was always attractive, but her passion for the art here made her beautiful.

I shake my head and let myself cry. I'm not sure what I'm crying for. I think I'm crying for myself, for this cursed planet, and for all those who had the misfortune to die here. I am glad I dug Talart out. I want them separated. He's mine. She knew that. He should have continued to love me. His copy should have continued to love me.

I stay away most of the day and return under a star filled sky. I am not surprised to see the buggy gone. My first thought is to leave before they return. If I stay any longer I'll only lose Frond all over again as he begins to fade. I couldn't bear that.

But will Talart's copy suddenly appear beside me once I obtain enough distance? I can't even guess at her reaction. Grateful? Angry? Terrified? It would be cruel for her to find out like that. I will tell them. I just need to find the courage.

I wait. When I hear the buggy return, I go outside. Sure enough the steel ship, minus the glass, is with them. As Frond backs the buggy into the cargo hold, I look across the flat landscape towards the city's dark silhouette and picture the old ghost in his robe coming across the scrub grass after it. Talart stands not far from me. She is paler but her lipstick is still bright and her hair, where it escapes from her hood, is still red.

I walk up into the cargo bay and watch Frond try to open his locker. He's finding it difficult. I clear my throat. He looks up at me. We maintain eye contact for a few seconds until he breaks it off. There is now no need to tell him anything. He already knows.

I want to comfort him somehow. I want to tell him that his eyes are still honey brown and that I still love him. I want to tell him we will always belong. But then again what does that mean? No matter where we are, what we do, who we love, we drift, always longing for something we don't have. Longing for an ancient world we never ever knew, except perhaps in reconstructed images of sailing ships and chariots.

Later, as the stars become milky with weight, I go searching for Talart. I stand close to her.

"I'm sorry about this morning," she says. "That was a horrible way for you to find out. We were going to tell you. It just all happened so fast."

"It's okay, Talart."

"I just want you to know," she says. "The last thing we ever wanted was to hurt you."

I close my eyes. But you did. You both did.

"I understand if you don't want anything to do with me or this art, but I plan to find a backer so I can return and salvage some of it."

She still doesn't know. Frond couldn't find the words either.

"And I'm splitting all profit with you and Frond. This is our find. Not just mine," Talart continues.

I smile then. "That's very generous of you. I'm not sure I would do the same. But what if Frond's right and it's just copies of her art that those old welding bots had in their data bank?"

She laughs. "Then they made damn good copies." She leans into me but I barely feel it. My heart sinks a little. I suddenly want more than anything for these two people to be alive and well so we can simply continue on.

"We thought we would go for one last walk under these stars. Would you like to join us?" she asks. She is sheepish as she says it, trying to gage my reaction. "Maybe together we can shake him from that mood he's in."

I shake my head.

She begins to walk away. I want to ask what I should do with her but all I can think to say is, "Is it good between you two?"

She nods.

"Did he show you the water tower yet?"

She turns around. "The what?"

Part of me is pleased that he kept this from her. "Ask him to show you."

She's mainly in shadow now but there is a flash of plum. I smile back.

I wait until they're gone before climbing into the cargo bay. I pull equipment away from the wall and yank on the container bag that holds Talart's body. In some ways I wish I didn't free her from the mine. This should not be my decision, but I can't leave Frond down here alone. He needs Talart. Just realizing this makes me feel unhinged. One moment I can't stand to see them trapped together, the next moment I'm facilitating it. I ignore my back and pull Talart from the ship. I pull her far enough across the scrub grass to hide her so they won't know that I was the one to trap her here.

I then climb back into the ship and ready it for departure. I keep wondering if they'll remain with each other even when they can no longer touch one another. I think back at the prostitute near the steelworks who continues to reenact the moments of her life, while her bones lay somewhere within the city's ruins.

I know nothing of salvaging. I know nothing of art, but I'll find out what I can about this sailing ship if only to find out its worth. If it's what Talart claims, I'll finance a return here to salvage both art and bones. Put some of these ghosts to rest.

The ship rises slowly and I fly low over the city, which is all velvet layers now, punctuated by tiny spots of light from broken bots. I think of those below, trapped, blending and breaking apart, irate and even-tempered, existing in a sub-existing state. I do one final bank over the plaza, and catch sight of Talart's steel horses pulling their chariot ceaselessly homeward.

☼ ☼ ☼

Mary J. Daley hails from Canada's east coast, lived in Toronto for many years, and now resides on a small farm north of the city. She is the mother of two wonderful daughters, and the owner of three dogs, one cat, and two rescued horses. Her publishing credits include Electric Spec, Fantastique Unfettered, Lore and others.

Mapping the Crooked Places

by Cameron Suey

When I emerged from a decade beneath the waves of my private sea, my parents were dead and gone. With a clarity I had not experienced since my youth, I drifted like an airborne seed through the City. I fell in love, not with my fellow man, but with the places men gather. With a small fortune, the life insurance and inheritance that churned the modest guilt inside me, I put down gossamer roots into a dozen places across San Francisco, staying only long enough to satisfy my curious new desire for belonging, before again taking to the breeze.

In every place I settled, I drew a map, dreamed a new metaphor. When I lived in the shadows of the medical college, haunting bars filled with sleep-deprived and wild-eyed doctors-to-be, my map of the City was like the organs and cells in a body. A vascular system of roads, a nervous system of wires, and the pale and textureless connective tissue between.

When I left the drafty Cole Valley flat for a studio loft in the Mission, I mapped the City as a battleground: isolated camps of combatants brought together by common ideals, surrounded by the rotting demilitarized zones of cultural vacancy.

From a top floor apartment on Market Street, I saw the City as a vast and productive farm, where I surveyed each field, growing signature and heirloom crops to be counted, stored, and sold. Like any farm, there were fallow places between the fields, cracked and rotting fences, and rusting abandoned machinery.

In every place I settled, these nameless in-between places, the featureless empty zones between the landmarks and neighborhoods filled me with shivering unease. Like minds without souls, the interstitial boroughs seemed on the verge of rotting away beneath my feet. It was many months before I could admit why.

They were the very places I had once sought out, grey places filled with grey faces, where I once found quiet oblivion without judgement. The empty hollows of civilization that I let suck so much of my life away. With the veil now lifted, I did everything I could to avoid them, and their whispering temptations.

Inside the vibrant neighborhoods where I now made my homes, I would travel only by foot or bike, for fear that I would wall myself away from the beauty. But when crossing the borderlands, I needed the barriers of taxi cabs and train cars. The empty places reeked of my disease and threatened to make me ill. I passed through them only when need dictated, and my resolve was strongest.

When my map of the City and her identities grew dense, I had still not found a place I felt I belonged, a place I would want to truly live in. I imagined, like the newborn that I was, that all the City's secrets were known to me and my love for her turned sour. I flirted with the idea of starting again, picking another of the world's great cities and emerging, naked and fresh into a yet another new life.

In a fugue of self-pity, I forgot why I feared the hinterlands between the hearts, and wandered into their blankness, again and again. I found outposts inside these places, where people gathered together for heat, for light, for company, defiant against the bleakness that surrounded them.

Although I could no more relate to them than I could the denizens of the more desirable neighbors, I found comfort in those places. Not the comfort I craved, but the comfort I remembered. It was there that I could crouch on the precipice, and peer back down into my old oubliette.

An old familiar voice whispered back from the darkness, and I began to think echoes of old thoughts. Perhaps I had ignored these places, and much of the City, so much of what truly made it, under false pretenses. I had allowed the weakness of my own character to cloak these misunderstood places in a miasma of fear. A fear that stemmed only from my own failings.

With renewed desire, I threw myself back into my exploration, to again be a cartographer. To map the crooked places that had once held me in a different kind of thrall. I could return to the shadowlands, and see them for what they really were, and I could pass through them unharmed and clear of mind, and continue my search.

This is what I told myself. I even believed it, some of the time.

It was on this last leg of my quest that I came upon the tower.

It stood alone, in a district that should have curled cold tendrils of unease around my spine. The streets were empty and clean, in a way that suggested not constant attention, but disuse, and its only neighbors were warehouses and the pale shadows of failing restaurants and cafes.

I had seen its skeleton from a dozen of my nests, for it had been growing all the while, like the twisting branches of a great stone and glass tree, for the last half of the decade. It should have filled me with loathing. Artless and empty, a featureless glass monolith designed to house the young and wealthy, and those who were drawn to the in-between places for all the wrong reasons.

But when I encountered it then, during that final phase of my exploration, something inside it tugged at me, hooked me like a fish and never let go. Something high above the city streets called out to me, singing to me alone. It was an old song, sung with a new voice. The sensation was so familiar that I was scarcely aware of the pull. It felt like coming home.

Nothing about the tower was beautiful. I see that now. But I had written a check, a deposit for one of the sterile condos above me, before I realized that I had walked inside.

In that familiar fog of desire, I knew one thing: I needed to be on the upper stories, for the song came from high above me. I convinced the corpulent building manager of my need and he cracked his wide grin, baring twin rows of perfectly straight teeth, and assigned me a unit on the top floor.

I rode the elevator in breathless anticipation, and went straight to my first room.

My belongings and possessions were brought to me later, for once I entered the tower, I only exited it once more, for good, nearly five months after. When I left, I was free of the fog, free of my crooked need to find the soul of the soulless places, free of my love of cities and the places of men. I was scoured clean, left raw and naked, every sensation amplified and painful. I left with only my terror and my life, although how much of that I retained is in question.

The first apartment's spacious and empty rooms still smelled of construction, dust, and antiseptic cleansers. One glass wall in each room offered a sprawling view of the bay and the crumbling docks, the last few vestiges of proper industry inside the City's borders.

I already understood that it was not the view that my sudden, hot desire for elevation demanded. It was something else. Within moments, I also understood this: the top floor was too high. Whatever I was drawn to was now beneath me.

I left the room and began to descend the stairwell, the metal steps still covered in powdered drywall. I felt the invisible draw in my lungs, in the beating of my heart, and in the crooked trail of scars on my arms. It took a few dozen floors before the locus of my attraction was level with me and I entered a hallway that looked identical to the one above.

My fingers drifted up to the eastern wall, without thought, as so many of my actions had once been, and would become again. I paced the hallway, and I felt a pull down the length of my arm. Like a dowsing rod, I dragged my fingertips across the rough texture. The hissing friction of fingers on plaster and my soft footsteps on the carpet were the only sounds. The air was redolent of paint and carpet glue, but beneath it all, dancing in the air like a cracking whip, was a thin thread of something sickly-sweet. A night blooming flower. A corpse on the border of rot. It was intoxicating.

I reached a door, halfway down the hall, and my legs froze as if rooted to the spot. On the other side of the heavy wooden door, just past my raw fingertips, lay the source of the call. I felt an intense, delicious anticipation, a nearly fulfilled desire, the calm that comes just before the pinprick.

No logic could explain nor language could describe what my mind yearned for, for although the sensations were familiar, the source of the song behind the door was fundamentally alien, and a thousand times stronger. The sweet ache took root in the very structure of my flesh, and throbbed with my heart. I raised both hands, fingers splayed wide in a lover's caress, and held my body to the cool wood of the door.

I had to enter the room. I needed to be inside. This could only be the home that I had been searching for.

I looked up to the numbers, 2319, picked out in delicate and filigreed gold numerals, and committed it to memory, repeating them breathlessly. I knew, with a sharp pang, that I would need to leave the doorway before I could return to be fulfilled. I would offer any price and pay any cost, but I would cross the threshold. I would go inside, and I would be made happy and whole.

I might have stayed fixed to that spot, almost but not yet touching my prize, forever. But after a long moment, through the warped glass bead of the peephole, light flared, shaking me from my trance.

It took me a fractured moment to understand. While I pressed my body to the door, sighing with private intimacy, the occupant of 2319, the interloper, had been on the other side, staring out.

What kindled in me then was not the polite embarrassment that good breeding and decency demanded, but something more akin to sexual jealousy. But there was more, a violence I felt boiling in my forearms and clenched fists. Something bestial, cruel.

Reason returned, and I relaxed, secure in the knowledge that I had the means and now the clarity to take what I needed in the proper way, with no need for bloodshed. I grinned into the looking glass, my eyes slitted with cold assurance.

I was not a man accustomed to being disappointed.

The manager, that perfect creature of the dead zones, merely furrowed his brows when I returned holding out my checkbook. The room was indeed taken; it was the first chosen, by the very first occupant. He made clumsy jokes at first, not seeing the clarity of my need.

Desire made me needle-sharp. I offered to buy out the occupant. I offered to buy the whole building. In the end, the best I could do was place my name first on a waiting list. In the meantime, I moved my deposit to a new room, 2219, where I could wait just below, and bide my time until the occupant could be persuaded.

I never unpacked, even though I had the contents of my previous beachside flat shipped to me at great expense. I lived out of boxes, on minimal furniture, and subsisted entirely on delivered food. 2219 was close enough to the wet and living beacon above me to act as a temporary salve, and for a while, I thought it might be enough. Simply being there filled me with a kind of contentedness that I had only dreamt of.

My previous life, the wandering cartography of the invisible borders was over, for I'd found what I had been searching for.

I would lie on the floor, eyes drifting between the floor-to-ceiling windows, and then to the neutral texture of the roof above, trying to see through. The City beyond held no meaning for me any longer. If I wished, I could still see the neighborhoods and districts I had loved. I could see the grey stripes of nothingness that bound them to each other, the no man's lands that I had tried to avoid. But I no longer saw.

I had misunderstood the City, and now I saw its true meaning. Every part of it, unknown and known, existed across centuries for one purpose: to birth the tower. To create the room above me to safely house the thing, whatever it was, that sang out in promise to me.

I could smell it in my waiting chamber. The strong floral scent permeated the walls, and stuck to my skin, cloying and thick. I heard harmonic vibrations, echoing through the walls, and down the wires, and into my veins. My whole life had led to this place and this time, and I hovered on the precipice, terrified to go any closer, for fear of losing it all.

But soon, proximity was not enough. I found myself standing on a wooden chair, sometimes for hours on end, trying only to be closer to It. I would stretch my arms high, and press my palms to the ceiling, feeling the siren song running down through carpals and radius and ulna and humerus and spreading into my lungs and heart, like a warm and familiar wave.

But even that could not sate me, so I coiled my desire and need into a sharpened point, and brought it to bear against the occupant, the silent intruder above me.

☼

I began with noise. I unpacked my stereo and pointed the speakers upward, blasting random and sharp intervals of atonal nonsense. The tower was still sparsely populated, in truth nearly empty. I knew that I had the floor to myself, and but a single neighbor above. Yet another sign I disregarded utterly, one in an endless parade that should have driven me far from the place, had I still retained my sanity.

But instead I squatted in that abominable and heartless husk of a home, in a place that should have set my teeth on edge. A wild-eyed and unrepentant fool, a quisling to all that I had claimed to love about the places of men.

When the occupant made no complaints, I raised the frequency, the volume, until finally I could no longer stand my own tortures. I turned to pounding on the roof with a broom, slamming the ceiling until chips of paint and plaster fell down into my eyes. More than once I thought of simply tunneling upwards, and emerging from the hole to choke the life from the occupant and claim my prize.

I got a response, at last. He would tap his heels, lightly, in echo and reply to my thundering, a retort I found mocking and intolerable.

I tried horrid smells, boiling foul and moldering scraps of food, and pouring them on the threshold of 2319 in the small hours of the morning. I made complaints against him, claiming he was responsible for the noises and the smells, but the manager believed none of it and threatened to expel me.

I began to slide notes beneath his door, angry volatile screeds, threats, grotesque descriptions of the violence I would visit upon him if he did not vacate the place. They became pleading, mewling cries, offers of wealth, lies and thin tales designed to stoke his sympathy for my needs. I had made a life, once, of manipulating people to achieve my desires, and now I used every tool at my disposal.

In the end, he would thrust the notes back out as soon as I slid them in. He was always in, always home, and I understood this. He, like myself and so few others, knew, felt the pull of the place and of whatever was inside. In my most magnanimous and clear-headed days, I knew that he and I were kindred, and he had merely had the luck of being first.

I grew thin, physically and mentally and I became brittle and dry. I was on the verge of giving up, not my desire for the special place above me, but of the very act of living in a final, childish tantrum. Although I was closer than I dared dream, the distance felt magnified, and I knew if I left, it would haunt me, a bullet lodged in my flesh, working its way toward my heart for the rest of my days.

At last, after a week of petulant fasting, it came to me that there were only a few paths left to lead me to what I needed. I pulled my ragged body, barefoot and reeking, from the sodden chair where I had sat for more than a day. From the kitchen, I retrieved the snub-nosed pistol that I had hoped never to need, and left my ersatz apartment. I shuffled on tingling legs towards the stairway, and began to climb.

I smelled the sweet-death smell on the air-conditioned breeze when I entered his hallway, and I pushed my shaking body toward the door. At the precipice, I hesitated, and considered moving straight to violence. I could blast the lock from the door, enter with or without permission, and still have enough bullets to clear the occupant from the equation. But I believed we both deserved one final, peaceful chance, and so I knocked.

And knocked again, and again. After a while, I heard him moving behind the door, a slithering sound like a snake, squatting in the place that should have belonged solely to me. But he would not answer, so I knocked as hard as my condition would allow. I pounded until my knuckles bled. I shrieked, and although the sound from my dry and cracked throat lacked the proper authority, I continued to scream as I hammered the door.

At last, I heard the sound of whispers, and the thought of the occupant speaking to It made me nauseous with jealousy. But then I heard him slide towards the door, and turn the handle. I wrapped my fingers around the cool assurance of the gun, a totem of my authority, should I need it.

The door opened, a fraction of an inch, and the occupant's gleaming eyes met mine. He opened it further, to the full extent the brass chain on the door would allow. I might have kicked against the door, forcing my way inside, but I held fast to some notion that I could still get what I wanted without the undue risk that violence would bring.

He was born to be citizen of the borderlands, like I had become. Plain and well groomed, he dressed in expensive clothes, worn comfortably like a second skin. Some may have called him handsome, but it was a flavorless sort of pleasantry, symmetrical, synthetic. The imprints of our shared passion clung to him, marking him as brother and nemesis.

He smiled at my wasting body, and the stained clothes that clung to my bony frame. But after every glance, I saw his black eyes snap backwards. Towards the locus of our need.

"I understand," he said at last, his eyes still fixed behind him. "I really do."

Despite my resolve, I began to cry. Small, exhausted sobs shook my body. If he noticed my shame, he pretended not to, whether in grace or embarrassment, I do not know.

"Soon," he said. The word hung in the air and coated me like a healing salve, pregnant with promise. "I'm afraid I'm done with It, or It with me. You'll understand."

He shook his head, a singular violent snap, and his face creased. It was a face unaccustomed to sharp emotions, looking oddly fetal and new, as something strong and sharp gripped him. He shuffled ever so slightly backward, his eyes fluttering behind toward the Thing I could not see. The knowledge that my desire, my prize, waited for me, just beyond his obscuring body clawed at me. My fingers twitched around the weight of the pistol.

"It waited so long for this place to be built," he said. "Patient. It was here before us, before the city, before anyone. And It will be here long after us."

Again he shuddered, and I saw the suit was soaked with sweat, far filthier than I had originally thought. Not creased, but wrinkled. I had somehow mistaken his tousled appearance for cleanliness, his chaos for order, but the glamour had faded. Beneath the night perfume of our mutual addiction, there was something else, something acrid and wrong. Panic, hysteria, terror. His calm and still demeanor, gone. A temporary posture, once wielded masterfully, he could no longer hold for more than a minute.

This was not my brother, no equal, I thought, as I steeled myself for what had to come. I knew, if I knew anything at all, the sight of a man on a precipice. And I knew how to push.

"You're right," I told him, and locked my eyes to his, stretching the last of my strength into a sharpened point. "It's going to kill you. It doesn't want you, and It's bored of you."

He opened his mouth, let it hang open like a fish. His eyes swam behind a veil of welling tears.

"I know ..." His voice was dry and papery, trash caught in the wind. "But I can't ... leave. Not yet. What makes you think you'll satisfy It?"

"It called to me," I said, stepping closer towards the gap, until I could smell his decay. "It called to me, and It has sung to me every night since I came. Like It no longer sings to you." I took this shot blind, but I saw in his wincing face that I had struck true.

"You might be right ..." he whispered with a joyless smile.

"That I'm here at all should cast out all doubt." I pressed further, putting one hand on the door to push back, until the chain vibrated and hummed. "Why are you making this so hard on yourself? It's time to go. It wants me."

At that moment, as if to harmonize with my argument, the sweet song behind him surged, hot and fragrant. We turned together, my gazes searching for the wondrous Thing that he alone could see.

"It's good to be able to talk with you," he said, after a long silence. "And you're right. You're right." He grinned wide, and I saw the rot in his teeth. "I needed this. To clear my head ... I think ..."

The words trailed off, and he turned, rocking on his heels. I threw my weight against the door with a feral scream, but his strength outmatched mine, and the door slammed shut with a click that sounded like the end of the world.

But then I heard the shuffle of his feet away from the door, heard him trying to hold his body aloft, before crumpling to the floor. I heard him cry out, a lost wail in the night from the very heart of our desire, and I knew that the gun would not be needed.

I had won, at last.

I returned to my room below with a lightness in my step that I had not felt since the days below the waves. I went to gather my things, and return. The time to submit myself to the Thing had come.

The muffled sounds of his voice, pleading and ragged, drifted down from above, and I grinned, approaching ecstasy. I heard the sound of something being dragged. There was a great surge of motion, announced in vibrations through the walls.

A treble explosion, a splintering symphony of glass.

Outside my window, a sparkling cloud of frozen light and an overstuffed leather chair hung illuminated in the night air. An absurd tableau of shattered glass and furniture, defying gravity. Then it was gone.

I heard, in the following silence, the heavy tread of his feet, and the meaningless babble of his final words. Away from the window, towards the door. Stop. A pacing circle. Stop. A sudden run, a blazing trail towards the window, towards the open night.

I pressed myself against the cool glass, the breath stopped in my lungs, and I saw him go.

One leg out, a runner jumping hurdles. Wild hair whipping in the breeze. Arms wide to the night sky. Free.

And like the glass and the chair before, he was gone. No sound announced his impact. He simply vanished.

The blooming corpse-flower smell surged, hotter and brighter than ever, and if I could have scaled the air itself to ascend to the roof above me, I would have clawed through, ground my fingers to the bone. But it was too much, and I broke. Each joint separating, each muscle going slack, I dropped to the floor, unconscious before I hit the ground.

☼

I woke, how much later I do not know, to the sound of faraway sirens trilling in the air. My body tapped into its final reserves, flooding my limbs with carefully hoarded fire, and I surged to my feet.

I didn't have much time: the police, the manager, they would be to his room any moment. I took the stairs two at a time, and flew down the hallway.

He had unlocked the door before his fall, in a final gesture of resignation. I put my hand on the doorknob, and sighed in glorious expectation as I pushed the door open.

The room was a twin of mine. The occupant, my predecessor, had lived like I had, out of boxes, with minimal furniture. Waste and rumpled piles of clothes were strewn across the room. The great hole in the glass window sucked at the air, the sounds of traffic and the world below came to me for the first time in months. The curtains fluttered, whipping like flags of surrender.

The call was stronger than ever before, and I closed the door behind me, my eyes vacant and searching.

It was here. The siren, the flower, the lure. At first, I could see nothing, but as I walked on uncertain, atrophied feet, I began, at last, to perceive It.

As I stepped sideways, it resolved from nothingness, like a sheet of paper seen first from the edge.

It was a seam in the world. A tear, a hot and colorless rend across space. Impossibly thin, yet gaping wide, It flared, achingly bright, in recognition of my awareness. The cloying smell flooded my nostrils, and twined around my ribs. The call was a fire in my pierced forearms, in my veins, and my ecstasy was complete.

It seemed to curl and whip, but It never moved. Alien colors and smells flooded from the maw. Somewhere, deep in the core of my body, I felt It reach inside and touch me. The wordless beckon of the past months resolved, like a picture snapping into focus, and It spoke to me.

I walked towards It, my hands outstretched. Weeping with joy, the heat of the thing seemed to reignite every nerve ending in my body. It made me whole, healed me, comforted me, washed over me like the old wave, and I knew I would never want for anything, never fear. I would be loved for all time.

It asked precious little in return.

I might have stepped into Its oceanic arms forever, might have been lost to Its promises, if something had not awoken in me then.

Perhaps my true self emerged, sober at last, lost to the vile chasm's draw so long ago. Perhaps it was only the unthinking panicked animal we all hold chained in our psyche. The runner, the fighter. Perhaps it was the echo of the occupant, his last act of defiance still rustling in the breeze with the shredded curtains.

I do not know. Whatever emerged, it took control at that moment.

I saw Its lies. I saw It, imprisoned in the sky, calling out. Filthy, reeking promises to those below, those attuned to the foul wavelength of the desire for oblivion. I saw delicate filaments of influence, coils of burning plasma, reaching down to the City below, infecting and cancerous. I saw them wrapping around the lights and hearts of men, choking, crushing. Hateful.

It was the borderlands. It was the name to my nameless fear of the dark places, in the city, and inside me.

It was, and It will always be. It would use me, bend me, break me. It already had. When I was done, no more use to It, I would be cast aside, and It would call, again.

I tugged for control of my body, a flesh and bone traitor that still approached this fragment of profane divinity. I pulled harder, and when my vessel cracked free of Its grip, I slid back into my skin, and allowed the animal instincts to guide my escape.

I stopped only long enough to kick, twice, at the dials of the expensive gas stove with one bare foot. The rotten-egg odor of gas began to twirl with the corpse-flower smell.

An hour later, I would marvel at the blood pooling in my shoe with every footstep as I fled the tower, and raced to the edge of the City, but not now. Now I felt nothing.

I do not remember descending the stairs. I entered my flat, and grabbed a single still-packed duffel bag and my long abandoned shoes.

It called to me from above, furious and reproachful, promising and threatening all at once, and painfully familiar. I could not shut It out, but I held tight to the image of the occupant, soaring gracefully through the air. Arms forever failing at the task of being wings, hanging in the night sky.

I would leave the tower in my own way, I thought, and this simple promise kept my body my own.

I lit my own gas stove before I went, and from a curling a strip of a discarded pizza box, I made a small torch which I held to the ragged ceiling. One of the tiny frayed holes, the legacy of my vandal idiocy, began to smolder.

I do not remember choosing to do this. I simply did, because it was, unlike everything else in the tower, unlike everything else I had done for a half of a year, right, in some profound way.

When I left, It no longer was promising anything but everlasting suffering and pain and submission. Yet I still wanted to go to It, still felt that elemental undertow. At the staircase, I very nearly went up, feeling some awful analog of gravity tugging me skyward.

It would have been so easy to go to It, to surrender myself to Its magnificent tides, but I hung frozen in the air with my predecessor, saw his final relief and escape, and made my body descend.

Out on the sidewalk, a pair of policeman interviewed the manager, jotting notes as the fat man wrung his perfectly groomed hands. He saw me coming, saw me wild-eyed and unkempt, and his piggish eyes narrowed into slits.

He thought I'd come, now, to claim my spot on the waiting list, to take ownership of the room. He thought me a grotesque monster, a murderer.

He opened his mouth to speak, and from above there came a great and terrible roar, a cacophony of cracking glass. A tongue of fire licked the night sky from the gaping hole in the tower's side. Glass began to rain, burning scraps of paper and clothing danced in the night sky. While all eyes were upturned, voices raised in confusion and distress, I turned and slipped away into the night.

They want me back, in the City, to answer questions. I know that any day they will come with a warrant, and drag me from my new home, to answer for what happened in the tower.

I know, of course, that I failed to kill It. I could never have even truly harmed It. At best, I kept others from It, for a short time. Perhaps I kept a single mad and passionate fool from falling into Its slick and sweet honey trap. This, and my own temporary safety are enough.

I also know, that even if they never find this cabin, never track down the twisting trail of money that allowed me to flee the City, even if I live to see a natural death, that I can never be free.

It has marked me. Forever. That salivating, sweet smell is ever in my nostrils. It never stops speaking, and I will see It in every crumbling barn, in every rusting skeleton of every abandoned car.

I saw Its writhing tendrils, growing and thickening across the City as I fled, saw them twine across the land, in every highway border town. I see them in every dying community I've passed through.

It is not quite here, yet, in the dark woods, in my isolation, my final home. But It will come.

It is a corrupting and spreading growth. It isolates, It squeezes, It chokes, It infects. If a lone cell should escape, then the refugee can only carry the contagion with him.

It is inside me. Someday, It will have me back.

I can only hope, in the end, that I will fight. That I will not go willingly. But I know that when It calls me home, at last, I will go without question. I will return to a City that has become one immense dead place, one massive, heartless hinterland.

I will answer for my small and meaningless act of rebellion.

But not today.

Today, at the very least, I remain free.

Today is enough.

Cameron Suey is a California native living in San Francisco with his wife and two children. He works as a writer in the games industry, most recently on "Rise of the Tomb Raider." His work has appeared on the *Pseudopod Podcast*, several anthologies including *Shadows over Main Street*, and was featured in the first issues of *Jamais Vu and Flapperhouse*. He can be found on the web at thejosefkstories.com, and on twitter as @josefkstories.

Oubliette

by S.R. Algernon

How can *they* feel guilt if they don't remember?

That question brought me to an interrogation room in the heart of the ruined High City, face to face with a bald man in an orange jumpsuit. I sat down and placed an envelope marked 7108 on the table. He watched me with hope in his eyes. My lab coat, which covered my sweater and most of my skirt, must have marked me as an authority, as someone who could make a difference.

I knew him only as 7108, the latest of my interviewees, but maybe I could publicize his experience and help him reconnect with his past. My parents had disappeared after the war; my inward, awkward emptiness didn't fit with the sweeping arc of history, but it felt at home here among the ruins.

Every schoolchild knew the official story. The Lowland Alliance had besieged and looted the domed High City, ending its dominance over the Lowlands and ushering in an age of peace.

The aftermath never made it into the textbooks. By the time the Lowland Alliance had captured the city, a neurotoxin from the city's chemical arsenal had spread through the city. The victorious commanders soon discovered that the neurotoxin scrambled autobiographical memory, stripping their soldiers of their identities as long as they remained within its dome. The neurotoxin, and the lingering remnants of the city's defenses, thwarted the reconstruction of the city as a conquered trophy.

Meanwhile, the Lowland Alliance had no use for the anarchists, zealots, traitors and malcontents who had been so essential in stoking resistance in the early stages of the war. The Lowland commanders solved both problems by bringing them together. They left the city to rot as a monument to failed tyranny and quietly left their troublesome citizens to wander its streets as inmates, their grievances and ambitions wiped away, or maybe hidden somewhere within their minds. Someone had to tell their stories, as much as the Lowland Alliance would like to forget.

How can they feel guilt if they don't remember?

The interrogation room smelled of dried blood and fresh perspiration. My filter mask guarded against the neurotoxin, but the past seeped into my mind regardless. Spackle covered the bullet holes without erasing them.

"Hey, Doc," asked 7108. His shaven head reflected the overhead lights. "Are you here to give me a psych exam?"

"I want to understand your experience. Is it all right if I ask you a few questions?"

The prisoner opened his mouth halfway. Did he pause because he had already forgotten my question or because nobody had asked his permission before? The guards who had thrown him in here might say I could do whatever I wanted with him, but my white coat carried with it a moral imperative of benevolence. First, do no harm.

"Okay, I guess."

According to my handwritten notes, 7108 had killed thirty four people by detonating twenty kilos of fertilizer in a subway station in one of the Lowland regional capitals.

"Do you know why you're here?"

7108 bit his lip in thought.

"I can't imagine. If I'd done something wrong, I'd remember it, wouldn't I?"

"Look at your wrist."

He pulled back the sleeve of his jumpsuit to reveal a dog tag, held to his wrist by a length of steel chain. Block lettering on the tag read 7108 TERROR-IST ACTS—HOMICIDE, along with a red light on either side—a sign that his sentence was not yet up.

The phrase popped into my head uninvited, like the refrain of a half-forgotten pop tune.

"I'm no criminal," said 7108. His smile faded. "Wait a minute. Are you with my attorney? Do you work for the people who locked me in here? Whose side are you on?"

"Whose side do you want me to be on?"

A curtain of blankness settled over his face.

"Why are you here, 7108? Who do you think is to blame? Does some remnant of your memory system remind you what you've done?"

The corners of his mouth tightened. He looked down. Was that guilt—if not a deep reflective remorse, at least a flicker of disembodied shame? That slight connection offered the hope of rehabilitation. Otherwise, what was the point of punishing him, except as a cautionary tale?

Prisoner 7108 shook his head.

"I know how you people work. I haven't done anything. You won't get a confession out of me."

"You have something to confess, don't you? Do you see the twisted metal in your dreams? The charred sign that says MIND THE GAP? The blood on the platform tiles?"

I handed him an eight by ten centimeter photograph of the rubble that I kept in the envelope. He took in the scene and tossed the picture onto the table with enough force to bend one of the corners.

"I didn't do this."

Would I cross the line by pressing further? Had he revoked consent by rejecting the picture? What difference did it make? He'd forget in a few minutes. Besides, why shouldn't he imagine the faces of his victims, just like I imagine …

Just like I can see the faces of my parents?

The word "parents" hung in my mind. It had a nice enough sound. *In loco parentis* was a curious phrase that reminded me of trains.

Think. Focus. Who are my parents?

Several parents came to mind—celebrities, women with strollers in parks, stoic gray-haired women laying wreaths on headstones. Men with children at their sides, waving flags of the Lowland Alliance. They were all parents. Were any of them mine?

The chain ends with you.

I linked the voice in my head with a middle-aged man with close-cropped hair and a thick mustache. He spoke with fondness and urgency, but I could not say for sure if he was talking to me, or if I had merely observed him speaking to someone else.

I ran my fingers over the surface of my filter mask. *I'm all right. I'm all right. I just need a little air.*

"Guard," I said. "I have to get out of here."

No one answered. This is a prison, right? Where are the guards?

I walked out, and 7108 called after me.

"Lady, come back. You look upset. Did I do something wrong?"

The hallway outside, and the spray-painted DEATH TO THE HIGH CITY on its wall, offered no answers.

"Guard! Someone, answer me."

A chill came over me, and a nauseated emptiness spread through my stomach. As I pulled my arms around myself, something metallic on my right wrist brushed against the opposite forearm. I pulled back the sleeve of my lab coat. A dog tag underneath, chained to my wrist like a bracelet, read 6983 CYBER-TERRORISM. The light beside the label was green.

I can leave whenever I want. After the neurotoxin leaves my system, memories would come back to me.

Memories of what? What could I have done? The thought of blacking out a city or bringing down an airliner or siphoning money to people like Prisoner 7801 repulsed me, but why was I here?

A thought, bereft of context like a newspaper blurb, took shape in my mind.

The checkpoints still stood at the entrance to the police headquarters. The Lowland Alliance commanders had promised that High City technology—spoils of war—would launch them into a new age, but the encryption had proven too tough to crack.

I walked until I found an exit sign and then followed that to the checkpoint. I studied the dead scanners and smashed security console on my way to the exit, but no nefarious schemes or technical knowledge sprang to mind. The holes in the wall where the old High City data ports were—before the Lowlanders ripped them out—evoked only a desire to download the latest news updates.

If I'm a cyber-terrorist, I'm not a very knowledgeable one.

The atrium beyond the checkpoint led to a wide doorway with tracks that had once supported a sliding door. The view of the outside, framed in the wide doorway like a movie scene, showed only a bombed-out building across the street. The ambient light from the geodesic dome, out of view but hanging over the city like the discarded husk of a molted beetle, cast the building in a palette of rusty gray.

I stepped outside, onto a flight of wide stone steps. The dome came into view above me. The jagged hole at its apex had the scale and ashen solemnity of an extinct volcano viewed from within.

What was supposed to happen now? That question stayed in my mind as I looked to the street past the foot of the stairs. Someone out there could help me. A young woman pushed a cart alongside a scrapheap at the base of the stairs. Maybe she had something to trade. A lump in a plastic bag at the front of her cart was about the size of a drone battery. People would trade just about anything for one of those at the market. They could keep the lights and heat on in one of the apartments for the better part of a year.

A man stood in the skeleton of a bus shelter and counted the change in his hand over and over. A medical drone would come for him if he stayed stuck in the mental loop long enough to dehydrate. Two men tussled over a yellow water jug in the entranceway to the burned-out building. The guards didn't tolerate violence out in the open. If the patrols or the cameras spotted them, a drone would swoop down and disperse them with a jet of tear gas.

Drones. Everywhere I looked, my mind drifted toward drones. I pulled them out of the scene without meaning to. *My subconscious must be waiting for a drone. The only way out is through the hole at the top of the dome.* Reluctantly, I lifted my gaze upward to the jagged opening. Each geodesic triangle grated against my nerves like a shark's tooth. The city had not been ugly, once.

Once, sunlight had streamed in from the circular opening between the lip of the dome and a landing platform that hung down from it. Viewed from below, the light formed a halo or aura around the underside of the platform. Trade ships and passenger ships docked on the obverse, sheltered from the winds, while shuttles flitted between the platform and ground level.

Why can't I rid myself of that memory? My lab coat gave me hope. I was a scientist, and I knew my own mind. The city must trigger loose memories. If I could find enough of them, I could drape them over my blank self, like dressing a mannequin in a store window.

Who am I? I projected the question out onto the city and waited for ripples to come back.

In the heyday of the High City, thousands of political prisoners and malcontents had climbed the steps of the police headquarters in shackles.

That much had been clear from the war crime tribunal's transcripts. I could have read them before my arrest.

Children went several blocks out of their way to avoid walking past police headquarters on their way to school. A ghost haunted the stone steps, they said. She stood each night, dressed in Sunday clothes and a fashionable hat. She held a photograph in her hand and waited for somebody to walk out.

How did I know that? How did I know that the violets in her hat matched the silk of her dress?

Alexa had cried when she heard the story. She had run to the bathroom and not come out for ten minutes.

"Come out, Alexa," Jacona had said. *"I promise not to tell stories like that anymore."*

The names Alexa and Jacona meant nothing. The story could have been a rumor, but how could I have learned it? The anecdote had a place somewhere on my mannequin self, but where?

A drone the size of a family car landed with a grating hum, like a mosquito descending to feed. A gull-wing door opened up on the side, revealing a compartment with a steel-frame bed. A familiar voice emanated from the speakers within.

"We're ready to take you home. Please enter the transport compartment and place your belongings in the storage compartment beneath the mattress."

"What?"

"You've served your sentence, 6983. Time to go."

Alexa's mother had been a historian. The police had found among her personal effects the text of an ancient compact between five of the most prominent Lowland factions. This text was often found, along with bomb-making materials, in terrorist training camps along the coast. The police arrived on a summer night in an unmarked van. Alexa never saw her again.

Jacona had not known this when she decided to tell the ghost story. People did not talk openly about such things, not even to their closest friends.

I stepped back from the drone.

"I'm no criminal. I can't leave, not until I can prove it."

"Maybe you're not. Maybe you're a scientist. The tag on your wrist could just be a ploy to help you relate to the prisoners. Why not go back home and share your findings with the world?"

"What the hell are you talking about?" said a different voice from the drone's speaker. It sounded farther from the microphone.

"Just play along, all right?" said the first voice, muffled, "so we can cross her off the list."

Was I a scientist? No. That didn't explain Alexa. I was something else. A cyber-terrorist? Not exactly.

I'm buried in this city, along with the Lowlander compact and a leaky repository of neurotoxic sludge.

"Don't make this hard. You're free."

"I …"

Frustration and warmed-over despair came to my lips. My throat tightened around my words.

"I don't want to," I said.

"Listen to me," said the guard. "We're not supposed to tell the prisoners any details of their incarceration except what's on the tag, but we don't know what to do with you anymore. It's been months since your tag went green. At first, we thought we'd just scoop you up into one of the drones and carry you across the bridge but … I don't know how, but you sensed it. You begged to stay here. You said the same thing you're telling us now, that you're not a prisoner and that you belong here. You stalked 7108 for weeks. We thought once you'd talked to him, you'd convince yourself it was time to go."

"I don't believe that."

They'll take me away like they did to Alexa's mother. Like they did to my mother? Was that right? Was I Alexa?

"Dammit," said the guard. "Listen to me. You aren't thinking straight. You've got to—"

"Stick to the protocol, Julius," said the second voice. "She isn't worth your career. The paperwork will come through. We'll scoop her up and fly her out. Then she won't be our problem."

"I can't do that," said the first guard. "I don't care what the Health Commission said. This place screws with your mind permanently. My uncle was at ground level under the dome just before the canisters blew. He hasn't been right since then, like he was always halfway in a dream. 6983 did her time. She doesn't deserve this."

"I'm staying here," I said. "I'm not leaving, and you can't make me."

"You have to understand that—settle down. I'll take care of this—whether you're a doctor or not, you've got to leave on schedule. Go home."

"If you're going to break the rules, Julius, just tranq her already. We don't have time for this."

I ran down the steps at an angle, behind the drone. In my peripheral vision, it lifted off and spun toward me.

Alexa and her brother Geraki knew of hiding places throughout the city. They would look for them when they missed their mother or when their father drank.

Underneath Berrin's bakery, a storeroom extends under the ground floor of the adjacent building. It connects to a parking garage under an adjoining building that stretched for a city block.

The names in these memories startled me. Even if I had studied the High

City as part of a research project, why would I know the name of some baker?

I kept the name Berrin in mind as I ran. I crossed the street, turned left, then right at the next block. Berrin's derelict bakery stood at the intersection. Loose tile, gravel, and glass crunched underfoot as I ran to the entrance. The sign out front was gone, along with the metal frame that had supported it, but the anchor points remained on the façade. The door frames had a lattice of wrought metal that retained their beauty despite being twisted out of shape on one corner. I opened the door. An errant bit of metal scraped the pavement. I froze at the sound. On the other side of the door, a man climbed down from a wooden shelf and brandished a broken wine bottle.

"This is my spot. If you want to stay here, you've got to pay."

He looked over my shoulder at the drone and he backed away without letting go of the bottle.

Where could I hide? Berrin's was off limits unless I wanted to find out what the squatter wanted as payment.

The stacks of the High City library spanned three city blocks and could hide a person for days. Every book ever written under the city dome had a place there. On the day the siege ended, the city council set it alight with incendiaries. Some parts of the building still smoldered.

"What are you trying to find?" asked a guard over the drone's speaker.

"I don't know," I said.

"Hey." The shrill voice, outside my field of view, brought to mind seagulls at the beach. The drone swiveled toward the sound just as a piece of cinderblock bounced off the rear stabilizer. Two men stood down the block in that direction, above an abandoned craps game and a half-eaten ration bar.

"Good shot," said one as he reached for a brick. "I'll bet that thing's full of food and water. All we've got to do is crack it open, like a nut."

The drone fired a tranquilizer dart and hit him just below the collarbone. The other one grabbed the ration bar and ran.

Better them than me. A few prisoners in the distance broke away from a gathering crowd to watch the spectacle. *A crowd—the drone might lose track of me there.* I ran toward its center and soon found myself in the market.

An armada of folding card tables and office furniture stretched across the sidewalk and two lanes of street. An assortment of junk and petty treasures filled every flat surface.

The market had only one clear rule: Never take anything from the tables without offering an acceptable trade to whoever stood next to it. I stopped at an air hockey table and sifted through costume jewelry and scrap metal.

I noticed a pendant with the letter A in ornate High City calligraphy. A could stand for Alexa. I flagged down a woman in a dusty button-down shirt and a pair of baggy cargo pants cinched tight at the waist. She smiled as I approached

"Can I have this?" I asked, holding up the pendant.

"What'll you trade for it?"

"How about my filter mask?"

"No good. It's cracked on the right side. I'd have made the trade if it worked, though."

I took off the lab coat and balled it up. Before I handed it over, I took a key card out of a pocket and slid it into the envelope marked 7108 for safekeeping. The key card read 1813.

The woman shook it out and checked the fabric for rips or stains. The tag on her wrist had a red light and read SECURITIES FRAUD.

"You've got a keen eye," I said. "By the way, do you know your name? It's not Alexa, is it?"

"Call me Sue. It's not the name I came in here with, but it seems to fit. I know my way around corporate and tort law. I know where to hide money off shore. It's funny that I can't remember where I learned that from. I just know. Sometimes a few digits of a bank account pop into my mind. I've got a feeling that they—whoever they are—left me to rot here while they took the cash for themselves. I'll bounce back from it, though. Somehow, I always do …" The sentence trailed off. "Want anything else?"

"Well, I've been on edge lately. I'm looking for something to protect myself with."

"Isn't everybody? With your build, a close-quarters weapon wouldn't deter anyone. More than likely, they'd just try to take it from you." She glanced around. "I think I see something here that would suit you."

She abandoned the air-hockey table, letting another prisoner take on her role, and led me to a coffee table. Mixed in with an assortment of plastic children's toys was a white pistol. Its oversize barrel had an indigo cloud insignia, the hallmark of a High City sidearm.

"It's a real plasma thrower. Too bad it doesn't work." Sue clicked the trigger a few times. "You could still scare someone with it, though."

"Can't I get a working one?"

Sue arched an eyebrow.

"I doubt you have anything worth that much."

"What do you want for this one, then?"

"What'ya got?"

"Nothing but the chain on my wrist," I said.

"I'll let you have it for the filter mask," she said. "I might be able to fix it up. A working mask around here would really be worth something. Almost as much as a working gun."

We swapped. I wrapped the gun in my sweater at the waistline, exposing the hem of a pink shirt underneath. By midday, the sun dissolved my tension. The memory of how I had acquired it had slipped away, but having it around allayed my fears. What was I afraid of?

"Come on, Jacki. You're not scared, are you? Berrin's gone for the day, and that idiot Kel is outside fighting with his girlfriend again. He's got the CLOSED sign up. Nobody will see."

"My parents are waiting for me. I have to go."

I closed my hand around the knob and then flinched as I noticed a man sleeping on the shelf where Berrin used to display custom cakes. He'd knock a tenth off the price for birthdays. I climbed in through the smashed picture window and searched the floor of the back room behind the register. The concrete walls had no breaks or seams. Old freezer units, now stripped of doors and shelves, occupied the far wall. A hint of rye hung in the air. I closed my eyes and plucked the odor from the background of dust and grime.

"Mr. Berrin has a secret room back there, full of money and who knows what else," said Alexa. She had pulled out two trays of cheese and butter and pushed on the panel behind her, which opened inward. Jacona stood in the storage room, beside racks full of rye and pumpernickel.

Jacona ran for the door with her shopping list in hand.

"Where's the bread, Jacki?" her mother had said, later that afternoon. "It was on your list."

"Berrin's was closed."

I opened the freezer. Hinges creaked and the smell of warm mold wafted through the air. I crouched in the empty freezer and pushed against the rear wall. It gave, but caught on something after a few centimeters. A smell reminiscent of acetone and ammonia drifted in through the opening.

"Hey!" Clothing rustled in the front room. Slow, asymmetrical footsteps followed; the even ones were louder and quicker than the odd ones.

I hunched down in the freezer and pushed against the back wall. Metal scraped against metal, and the door moved a bit more. Almost there.

The squatter appeared in the doorway with a broken bottle in his hand. Locks of hair hung in front of his eyes. He wheezed with each inhalation and swayed with each step forward. "This place is mine. Clear out or I'll slit your throat."

"Leave me alone. I didn't do anything to you."

I aimed the gun at his chest.

"Is that a toy? Put that down, girl."

"It's not. It's real." The petulance in my voice startled me, as I looked up at the squatter from a child's height.

The squatter reached down for the barrel. My fingers tightened around the grip. The trigger clicked. A flash whited out my vision for a moment.

I waited with my eyes closed for the squatter to take hold of my wrist and drag me from the freezer. He never touched me. He never made a sound. Something fell against the tile, and I opened my eyes.

The squatter lay on his back, with his head and shoulders propped up against the far wall. His abdomen and half of his ribcage on his right hand side were gone. What remained of his chest twitched without rising or falling. The pallor in his face had deepened and took on a blue tinge.

The hum of a drone outside broke the silence.

I tossed the gun and pulled my arms and legs into the freezer.

I can't go out now. They'll know what I did. They'll find me. The metal edge of the dog tag scraped against the wall. Its green light stood out against the darkness of the freezer.

I know what that means. I can leave anytime I want.

No. Not anymore. They'll turn the tag red when they see what I've done. They'll etch HOMICIDE onto the tag and send me back here.

He deserved it. He said he'd slit my throat. I crawled out and checked his right wrist, expecting to find a chain and a tag reading KIDNAPPING, RAPE or HOMICIDE.

His wrist was bare. Above it, on his forearm, a tattoo showed the names ANNA and KEL intertwined within a heart.

"Kel gets winded easy," said Alexa. *"They say he's unfit to serve in the Guard. I saw the other boys ribbing him about it. When Anna comes by, he'll*

pick a fight with her. That'll be our chance. Come on. I'll show you something we're not supposed to see."

All right, Alexa. Show me. Anything is better than here. I picked up the gun and gave the back panel a hard kick and it gave way. Beyond it was a staircase within a dusty, cavernous room. I ran down the staircase and felt my legs give out on the second to last step. As I stumbled forward, my stomach spasmed. I swallowed. My next breath burned. I coughed, which sent my stomach going again. The urge to vomit sent me to my hands and knees. The wet grating sound of retching filled the room.

"Come on, Jacki. Slowpoke."

I heard a giggle somewhere in the distance.

My head swam as I rose to my feet.

Where was I? The odor in my nostrils triggered a dry shred of memory.

High City defoliants and chemical weapons sank in air. They collected in valleys after each counterinsurgency operation, stripping the Lowlands of scarce arable lands. Residents of the High City could always pay the rising cost for fruit and grain.

Two strongboxes lay on their side. The locking mechanisms were gone, and the metal was twisted out of shape around the latch, but piles of turquoise polymer bills, High City currency, lay on the floor. Sacks of flour lay unopened, except where the rats had chewed through them.

Rats will only eat a small amount of any food with an unfamiliar taste. If the food sickens them, they will avoid it in the future.

My eyes burned and watered. Phlegm gathered painfully in my lungs. My arms felt heavy.

Let me rest, just for just a little while.

I leaned against the flour, coughed and vomited again. On the ground behind them, I saw a purple, bloated form wrapped in a white uniform lay behind the sacks.

Berrin offered discounts on bread and muffins on Sundays, and on festival days he donated all of his day-old bread to hungry children in the Lowlands. He had a new model truck every year—white with blue lettering—and it appeared without fail in all the official city parades.

He must have thought he was safe, and that he could ride out the siege with food and money to spare. If the chemical storage tanks had withstood the siege, he might have.

High City concrete has long been prized for its toughness. It withstood two months of bombardment. Rumor had it that the city council had detonated the chemical weapons on purpose, to give their partisans a chance to seek shelter in the confusion.

What did the city council have to do with anything? I stared at the floor, eyes unfocused.

High City concrete contained pumice quarried from mountains that were inaccessible without the aid of an airship.

Where was I?

I looked up and saw a ladder on the far wall, leading to a padlocked trap door.

The year before the siege, Councilor Kern addressed the council to denounce the Lowland food riots as a terrorist conspiracy. "We cannot allow them to drag us down into barbarity. The greatness and power of the cosmos lay just beyond our grasp. The choice is ours. Climb or die."

My arms floated as I aimed the gun. I shot out the padlock and then the hinges. The square metal door clattered to the ground. The sound triggered a new wave of nausea.

Light floated in from above. Light meant air.

I climbed the ladder and found myself in an open paved space, maybe a parking garage. I coughed for what felt like hours, vomited twice more, and curled up, shivering, on the asphalt and passed out.

In dreams, I chased after Alexa. In those dreams, I saw her face and felt a flash of visceral familiarity, but each time the face was different and the details faded away.

I awoke the next morning. My skirt was stained gray from where I had lain on the pavement and dusty brown at the knees, but I could live with that. My sweater stank from the flecks of vomit on the front, so I took it off. The chain on my wrist snagged on the fabric.

It's green. I can leave whenever I want. The thought filled me with dread.

Underneath the sweater was a faded pink tunic with a torn seam at the right soldier. The fabric felt like thick silk. I knew I would need more than that by nightfall, unless I found shelter first.

The unfamiliar cityscape confused me at first, until by chance I saw police headquarters.

The children used to go blocks out of their way to avoid the police head-

quarters on their way home from school.

I knelt down on the sidewalk. The child's-eye view triggered a jolt of terror that permeated the air, like the pheromone trails that ants follow. I let my intuition take me the rest of the way. Eventually, I stopped at an apartment building that seemed tall enough to give me a view out over the water. I walked through the revolving doors and tried the elevator. I pressed the only button that still had a readable floor number—1°.

18?

Across from the elevator lobby, I found my apartment and, by habit, pressed my hand against a panel beside the door.

"Welcome home," said the panel. The door unlocked.

I saw a computer panel near the door with the faceplate removed. Wires stretched down from it to a drone battery that rested on the floor beneath it.

"Computer," I said. "Do I have any messages?"

Who would call me here? How long had it been since this wreck of a building had a real tenant?

I promise I'll write, Jacki.

It couldn't hurt to check, could it?

"The city network is unavailable. Please try again later."

It was worth a shot.

Remember, the chain ends with you.

I was here for a reason. I looked around the room with a sudden sense of urgency. An instant camera on a dresser caught my eye, along with the half-dozen eight by ten centimeter pictures of the city next to it. I picked up the camera and turned it over. The side had a printer slot, and someone had etched the letters JT in the corner. J.T. stood for Jacona Trexis.

This was mine, but how did it get here?

As I lifted the viewfinder to my eye, the green light on my wrist caught my eye.

I can leave whenever I want.

But how did I get here? I must have done something terrible, too terrible even to contemplate. What was it? What was my sentence? What had I done?

Thirty four people died in the Lowlands at a train station in a regional capital.

No. That wasn't it.

Clear out or I'll slit your throat.

I must have done something. Think.

I'm sorry, Alexa. Come out. I won't tell that story anymore.

The clothes slipped from the mannequin faster than I could find new ones. They didn't fit.

Heavier than air defoliants from counterinsurgency campaigns collected in Lowland valleys, exacerbating an already worsening famine.

That wasn't my fault. Even if I did live here, I wasn't responsible for deployment of chemical weapons in the Lowlands.

Was I?

Wait. That's it! The toxins sink in the air. I walked to the window, aimed my camera at the dome's surface and zoomed in. Against the backdrop of the geodesic triangles, a finer web of ladders and catwalks stretched to the battle scars at the top.

If I could climb up there, the memories would come back. I snapped a picture of the ladder. The print fluttered to the floor. I picked it up and held it out in front of me like a lure as I sprinted down the stairs. The air scratched my throat and my lungs floated in a warm ache. I took the steps two at a time and pushed off the wall at each landing. Looking up from the screen only when I had to, to keep from crashing into a pillar or tripping over rubble. The prisoners either stared at me blankly or ran for cover and watched the skies. A drone joined them. It watched from the alleys, its headlights shining in the shadows like cats' eyes.

The city gave way to a ring of overgrown parkland. Beyond that, the bottom fifty meters of the dome's edge sloped inward as its base thickened. Graffiti at the base read DEATH TO THE HIGH CITY and JUSTICE AT LAST. Every half kilometer, a scalloped alcove within the dome's base held a steel door. Access hatches two hundred meters above the doors opened onto the scaffolding.

There must be a staircase inside.

I ran to the nearest door. The handle turned but the door did not open.

A drone pulled up behind me and hovered three meters above the ground. Its headlights lit the alcove's shadow, revealing the discoloration at the doors edges, scars from a welder's torch.

Of course. Why would they leave the doors unlocked in a prison? There has to be at least one weak spot. They couldn't have sealed the whole thing up, could they?

"Are you looking for a way out?" said a voice from the drone's speaker. "You're free to go, any time you want."

"Go to hell. I don't need you."

"Let her waste her time if she wants to," said another voice from the drone. "Just pick her up when she runs out of steam. In the meantime, there's a food drop by the pumping station in fifteen minutes. Get on it."

The drone ascended and veered off.

This was my city. Once, I must have known the way out, if I could only remember ....

I ran along the dome's inner circumference, kneeling at every storm grate. None of them budged. I ran my eyes along the curve of the dome until I found a pile of rubble that abutted the wall. If it were too much trouble to clear, they might have not bothered to weld it shut.

My sluggish thighs and ragged lungs complained at each step, but slowing down meant stopping, and stopping meant settling down to rest. Night would fall, and the next day would bring the same meaningless wander through the city. Sleep would wash the insights away, leaving useless hunches and long-ings.

I climbed over the rubble of a tram station. The remains of a passenger shelter and ticket booth had obscured the metal door. A charred sign read MIND THE GAP. I pushed some of the rubble aside, turned the handle and pulled. The door moved just enough to tell me that the latch was the only thing holding it in place.

The guards alighted here. They went to the outside of the dome and looked out over the lowlands. A girl stood on tiptoes to see over the railing and waved her pudgy arms as her father tapped in the access code and walked through the metal door. Her name was Jacona.

Maybe it was just a story or a rumor I had heard, but who tells stories about tram stations?

I tapped on the keypad, hoping my subconscious would reconstruct the sequence. The keypad did not respond.

It isn't over. It can't be. I ran my hand along the smooth metal, hoping for a handhold. I might as well try to flap my arms and fly.

It wasn't fair. I didn't want to leave. I let the picture fall from my hands, leaned against the wall and slid to the ground beside it. My head swam. My eyes stung as I looked up at the sun. The clear sky at the top of the dome blurred into an aura and then a halo. I imagined the landing platform and all the shuttles floating up to dock with the vast airships above it.

Late afternoon became twilight and I refused to rest. The drones left for the night, their tail-lights like embers rising from a campfire. By force of will, I saw instead High City shuttles, floating up from our skyscrapers to dock with a waiting airship on the landing platform.

"I'm staying here," I said. "I'm not leaving and you can't make me."

I folded my arms, the closest thing to defiance I could manage.

I fell asleep amid the rubble and dreamt of sirens, smoke and flame.

"I'm staying here. I'm not leaving and you can't make me."

"Come on now, Jacki. We can't wait. The defensive line won't hold for more than another few days."

"I thought the walls would keep the Lowland armies out. That's what they said in school."

"We can't hold out against all the factions at once. The Lowlanders have a leader now. He's promised the people down there that they'll split the City's wealth amongst themselves once they take it."

"If they come here, why don't we fight?"

"We will, and then in a while we'll come back for you."

I must have looked scared at that point, because he looked down at me.

"We'll find you after this is all over. Don't worry."

"I want to stay with you. I want to fight."

"You will, one day." My father paused. "You want to help, do you?"

"Of course I do."

"How about this? If you promise to get on the next ship out without complaining, I'll take you up to the fortifications on the outside of the dome. I'll show you the turrets. You'll see that we'll retake the city in no time, even if they break through. We'll put up a good fight."

"But you said children weren't allowed in the guard towers."

"Would you give your life for this city, if you had to?"

"Yes."

"Then you aren't a child. Come with me, Jacki. I want you to see it for yourself."

While you can, was the unspoken message.

I awoke some time later, contented. My stomach rumbled and my neck ached, but I was where I needed to be. I just had to wait. He would come back.

The ghost stood each night, dressed in Sunday clothes and a fashionable hat. She held a photograph in her hand and waited for somebody to walk out.

At midday, a familiar prisoner approached, still in his orange jumpsuit. He held an eight by ten centimeter photo in his hands.

"I've been looking for this place. I thought if I could find it, I'd know what the photo meant, but I still don't."

"I don't know what to tell you," I said. "I've never seen that photo before."

"It's all right. Do you have anything to eat? I've been walking all day."

"There might be some food behind this door. People from the High City sometimes hid food and money in out of the way places, so that they could retrieve it when they returned. Do you know anything about explosives?"

"Why would I?"

"Just figured I'd ask. This door isn't welded shut. If we could blow open the latch, we might find food in there."

"Maybe," he said, looking around. He spotted a spent shell casing. "If we had some ammunition I could think of something. Maybe a battery, too. I don't know, but I'll know what I need when I see it. Do you suppose I worked in demolitions before I came here?"

"I don't know," I said, speaking quickly before we lost our trains of thought. "Keep repeating the list out loud and don't stop, even for a second."

I kept the idea in mind and we walked. My intuition led us eventually to Sue and her fleet of tables.

"Hi there," said Sue. "Can I interest you a lab coat?"

"Not today. My friend is looking for supplies to make... what was it? Maybe some sort of bomb?"

Prisoner 7108 repeated his list.

"That's quite a lot," said Sue. "What'll you trade for it?"

"I don't have anything," I said. "But I'll give you a share of whatever we find."

"That's against the rules," said Sue. "At least I think it is. What the hell. Every investment has its risks, right?"

"Sure," I said.

Sue had a keen eye. Prisoner 7108 kept his mantra going while Sue worked the table. Within an hour, we had everything we needed. Prisoner 7108 carried it back to the old tram station. Sue watched for drones while the 7108 rigged the explosive.

The explosion was small, in terms of what the Oubliette had endured, but the door opened after a few persistent tugs. A rubber seal squeaked against the door frame as it opened.

"This is it," I said. "Come on and smell the air. It's different."

"Maybe there's no toxin in there. Out of the way, big guy. Let me in there. I've got to get my head clear and I can find an outside line. God knows what's happened to my portfolio in all this time. Those sons of bitches—"

Sue slumped forward. A tranquillizer dart protruded from her back.

"Drones," said 7108.

"Follow me."

I stepped into a metal corridor with exposed girders. The path ahead was a narrow bridge with a railing on each side. It stretched between the outer wall and a steel door. The hum of machinery echoed in the chasm below.

This part of the city still lived. My parents could be on the other side of that door, welcoming me back after a long, long day's work. I ran across the bridge, feeling just as small as I had all those years ago. At the halfway point. I turned back, expecting to see Prisoner beside me. Instead he stood, leaning against the railing and stared.

"What's wrong?" I asked.

"Thirty four people are dead because of me. It wasn't supposed to happen. Our target was a meeting of loyalist sympathizers at a local restaurant. They used to meet there once a week, every Saturday at eight. Every week, they reserved the main banquet hall. It was their routine. We had a man on the inside to get us past security. All I had to do was place the explosives and leave."

He stared into the darkness beneath him.

"That one week, they didn't meet at eight. They met at seven because they had a rally across town. By the time the bomb went off, ordinary hard-working families had just sat down to eat. I know because I hid in the crowd and watched from the street as the faction militia pulled the bodies out.

"Wait …"

I stopped. What was his name?

"I did what I had to do. I had my orders. Someone else would have done it if I had refused. Why do I deserve all the blame? Why do I have to see those burned-up faces in my dreams? It isn't fair."

He lifted one foot onto the railing.

"Wait," I said. "I need you. Sue needs you. The drones will get her. She needs your help."

"Sue?" He stepped back from the railing and turned toward me. "I don't owe her a damned thing. The only reason she helped us was to get a share of the profits. They sold us out to those High City parasites. They bled us dry, year after year, and they always got their cut. What did we get?"

I got ten percent off a custom cake for my eleventh birthday, a pink one with starfish on it. My father said that I'd earned it on account of my grades that year. Didn't I? Prisoner 7108 wouldn't see it that way. To him I'd be another parasite.

Whose side are you on?

He had asked me that question in the interrogation room. The sides mattered to him. As the memories came back, he'd recognize my silken tunic and see me for who I was. Isn't that always how it is with the Lowlanders?

"They have rage but no purpose," my father had told me, as I looked through his binoculars at the blasted shoreline dotted with a patchwork of farms and shantytowns. "The children threw rocks at the tractors. The men fired rockets from the rooftops. They wouldn't know what to do with the city if they had it."

It would be so easy for him to toss me over the railing. He wouldn't have to do it on purpose, just a shove in an instant of rage. He might feel bad about it later, but I'd still be dead.

Just like Kel.

I backed away from 7108. The metal railing chilled my back.

"What is it?" he asked. "What's wrong?"

What could I say to him, to make him leave me alone before he discovered who I really was?

"You're not ready to leave yet."

"What do you mean?"

"Look at your wrist," I said. "The light's still red. Did you ever think that maybe that light means more than some arbitrary sentence? Maybe it's a message to us, to warn us if we haven't discovered ourselves yet. The city is like a scaffold for our memories, or a plaster cast. It lets us rearrange them and reexamine them, without our past getting in the way. Go back to the tram station. Find Sue and help her. Then you'll find something worth living for. By the time they fly you out of the city, you'll know how to make things right."

"Maybe," said 7108. "Maybe I need to forget for a while. If you find any ration bars, will you bring them out for me?"

"Sure."

He turned away from me. I watched him go until I heard the door shut behind him, turned back toward the security checkpoint and walked the length of the catwalk alone.

After fifty meters, the corridor ended at a door and a row of scanners. Scratches and pry marks surrounded the door frame and the scanners, but the machinery still seemed intact.

I've been here before. My father was at my side, and I had to reach just a bit higher to put my hand on the scanner.

"DNA and handprint extrapolation confirmed. State your name to confirm voiceprint."

"Jacona Trexis."

"Match within system parameters. Welcome back, Jacona."

The door opened with a hiss.

I stepped into a room lined with empty metal racks. A bloodied dress jacket lay on the floor next to a broken helmet. A sign on the far side of the room read "Personnel must have defense clearance beyond this point."

"Don't worry," my father had said. "You're a guard now. Do you promise to do what I tell you? I'm your superior officer now, not just your father. You have to follow the chain of command."

The chain ends with you.

"Computer, do I have defense clearance?"

"Yes."

"What is my rank within the chain of command?"

"Your rank is 001. By the laws of succession, in the absence of a council directive, you are commander in chief of the city defense forces."

Succession would only take place if a superior were confirmed to be killed or incapacitated.

"Computer. Access the employee photos of Alan and Skye Trexis."

The memory of the mustachioed man waited in the back of my mind, just out of reach. If I fought back the lingering effects of the neurotoxin, his orders would come back to me. I wanted to see my parents' faces one more time first.

"Security lockdown is in effect, following breach of the city dome. Archival information is only available from the main security station via hardline transmission."

"All right. Can you display the route to the main station?"

The route wound through the wall's interior and sloped down, more than a hundred meters below the city.

The chain ends with you, a voice reminded me. A mustachioed man had explained it to me once. *You have full access to the city defenses. You must deliver the destruct command personally. This was the last military directive. If we cannot hold the city, we must destroy it before our enemies can break the encryption and take control of the weapons systems.*

I must have misremembered. The city had endured for so long. The Lowland Alliance must want to see it crumble to dust. The city council wouldn't destroy it, not unless there was no hope at all.

The chain ends with you, Jacona. You have to destroy the city.

Everyone else was dead. The Lowlanders had offered no quarter and no surrender terms. What would they do with the city if they could bring the old weapons systems online? Whoever controlled prison security could make a bid for power and rain devastation onto their enemies in the Lowlands.

Sue would die, and so would 7108, but how many more would be saved?

I found a data pod on a desk and plugged it physically into the security console. We had used them all the time at school. Their quantum storage meant that even the smaller ones could store the city archive with room to spare. The High City insignia appeared on the pod's screen as it turned on.

"Computer. Transfer the personnel files for Alan and Sky Trexis."

"Authorization accepted. Decrypting and transferring now."

The console flashed a green light to indicate a successful transfer. I thought of the chain around my wrist. CYBER-TERRORISM

"Computer. Check the security log. Were there any attempts to access the self-destruct sequence remotely using my biometric data?"

"Yes. One. Two point three years ago. Do you need a report?"

"No." No more stalling. It had to be done.

"Computer. Activate the self-destruct sequence."

"Stop," said a familiar voice behind me. I turned to see a man with slicked-back hair, who was shorter and thinner than he had seemed through the intercom.

"Julius?" I said. "That's your name right?"

"Destruct sequence to activate with fifteen minute countdown pending confirmation. Confirm?"

"You shouldn't be here," said Julius. "You're not a soldier. You're not even a terrorist. I saw you back at the police headquarters. You don't have the expertise to hack a military database. Somebody set you up, 6983. Go home. When your head clears, you'll realize they're using you."

"This is my city. I won't let you use it in your wars. Computer, can the order be rescinded?"

"Within five minutes of detonation."

Detonation. Did that mean a controlled demolition or a blast that would take down the mountainside? 7108 knew about explosives. Why couldn't he have toughed it out?

He would have said that there are hundreds of people in the city. Whatever the Lowland Factions did with the city's defenses would be their crimes, but the blame for those hundreds would be mine.

What if he were wrong? What if killing hundreds saved thousands or tens of thousands.

"Base, this is Julius. I need backup to …"

"Turn off your link," I said.

"Why?

"Do it."

Julius tapped behind his right ear.

"All right. It's done. What difference does it make? I can't force you to abort the sequence."

"They wouldn't have sent just one guard to investigate a security breach down here. They don't know I'm in here yet. As far as they know, you're on patrol. If they start looking, they'll find out I activated the system. They'll force me to transfer authorization to them. Whoever gets to me first will turn the city's defenses against its rivals."

"We—" began Julius. He stopped short, but I could finish the sentence. We're not like that.

"Maybe you're not, Julian. If you were, you'd be on the front lines some-where. Your people are better off without this city. All it does now is remind your people of when they were weak. You saw what 7801 did with a pile of fertilizer. What would he do with a fusion bomb?"

"I don't know. It doesn't matter. I still have to report you. I can't let you do this on my watch."

What if you didn't have to?

"Listen, Julius. I might be able to set the timer for longer, maybe fifteen days instead of minutes. You could go on leave. You wouldn't have to be here when it happened. You could shoot me right now and tell your CO whatever you want. You could say you killed the last of the natural born High City dwellers. They'd give you a medal."

Julius lowered the gun.

"I can't. My uncle stormed the dome after the siege. He was the hero in the family. He flew into that cloud of toxic debris, destroyed three gun emplacements and sent one of your warships into the mountainside. We show him the medals sometimes and tell him the stories because he doesn't remember any of it except in his nightmares. I can live without being a hero, but I'm no traitor. I can't let you destroy the city, not when there's a chance we could do some good with it."

"Then we'll stand here," I said, "while the countdown ticks away."

"This was easier," said Julius, "out there, when you were a nobody. Hell, I was a nobody too. I sat on my ass and guarded a ruin. I wish I hadn't looked so hard for you. We would have found out eventually and maybe had time to evacuate the city. My cousins would have made me the butt of jokes at every holiday. Now that I know, I have to try to stop you."

"Now that you know .... What would you do if you weren't a guard? What if you were under the dome right now, without a mask?"

"I don't know. I shouldn't say this, but I would be glad to see the City burn. I remember when I was a kid, I could see it glittering in the sunlight from my bedroom window. I saw the airships float down from it to spray the forests or dropped bombs. I used to think that the city made you evil, and that if we took it away from us, you'd change. You'd be like us. Instead ... I don't know. Sometimes I feel like we've turned into you."

Self-loathing dripped from his last sentence. Was it so bad to be us, to have philosophy and culture, and to reach for the stars?

"What are you thinking?" asked Julius.

"I don't know yet, but there are, what, hundreds of people here that your people are ready to forget about. They have nothing better to do. Why not give them something to work for? Why not set them to work rebuilding the city?

They wouldn't remember their old agendas."

"How? They have no memory."

"I can give them one." I said. "Computer, transfer all cultural, medical and non-military scientific texts to this pod. Include all civilian maps and directories for the High City."

"Done."

"With this information, I can bring the city directory and the archives back online. If your people get to know the city the way we did, not as victims but as builders, you'll know why we built it in the first place. It was never supposed to be a prize to fight over. It was supposed to inspire us. When your convicts finish their sentence, they'll bring back what they've learned and they'll use it to redeem themselves."

"I think the other guards will catch on," said Julius, "and what happens when the prisoners get out? They'll tell everyone that the City is back online. The factions will fight each other for the spoils and tear the City apart."

"By then, I think things will have changed. I've seen those convicts, from all walks of life. They work together because there's nothing telling them not to. Once they've gotten used to thinking that way, they'll use what they've learned here to make their lives better. They wouldn't ruin everything for the sake of some faction."

"So, you're not going to destroy the city?" said Julius.

"I guess not. Computer, cancel self-destruct order."

CANCELLED.

Julius stared blankly for a moment.

"And delete account JACONA TREXIS."

CONFIRM DELETION.

"Confirm," I said, hurriedly, before Julius had a chance to think of a way to stop me.

"There," I said. "Now I'm nobody."

"Same here," said Julius, following suit. "It looks like I won't have any good stories to tell my cousins this year."

"So," I said, "does this mean that nobody saw me?"

"If the other guards ask," said Julius, "I'll tell them that I searched the area thoroughly and nobody was here. You can count on it."

We shook hands.

On my way out, I wrote a note on the side of the data pod with a sharpie from the locker room.

UPLOAD TO PUBLIC NETWORK

As a precaution, I pulled a picture of the city map from the archives, marked it with a DO NOT DELETE warning on the bottom and left it onscreen.

The rubber seal scraped against metal as I opened the exterior door and walked onto the wrecked tram platform. My memories quietly, painlessly slipped away, but it didn't matter. I knew who I was.

S. R. Algernon studied fiction writing at the University of North Carolina at Chapel Hill and currently lives in Singapore. Work by S. R. Algernon can be found in publications such as *Nature*, *Daily Science Fiction*, and *Stupefying Stories*.

Mining Chernobyl

by Oren Hammerquist

"You ready for your first flatline trip?" Wilkinson asked the new miners.

"Flatline?" a nervous eighteen-year-old asked. "Why do you call it that? I thought it was FTL jump."

"Faster than light air travel liner: flatline. Don't worry, you'll understand what it means in a few minutes," Wilkinson said. "FTL jump is just what they call it when they want people to feel comfortable about it."

Radley Pond smiled at his old friend. Scaring the rookies was Wilkinson's unofficial job. Actually, it was more of a pastime, and all of the veteran miners did it. Wilkinson was just the best at it.

Radley always began with a short speech before the jump. "Let me remind all of you what you have gotten yourselves into. We are traveling to what remains of Earth. The buildings were largely undamaged by the radiation that wiped out the population, and we are going there to rip out what metal we can from what is left standing—large amounts of copper, aluminum and steel. Since this metal is already refined, it is highly profitable. Every available deposit of ore on the planet has already been mined. We are going to rob their tombs, and profit from the death of a civilization. If your radiation shielding fails, you will die. If your suit loses air pressure, you will die. Statistically speaking, at least one of you will not come back from this alive. If you pay attention, we may beat the odds. "

One of the recruits asked, "Are you trying to talk us out of going?"

"I'm saying you'd be stupid to stay," Radley said. "You've got about thirty seconds before the last escort ship disconnects. Say the word, we'll put you through the airlock."

"He means alive," Wilkinson said. "Not into space."

No one spoke, and there was a sudden sound of machinery. "Too late now," Radley said. "If this is your first jump, don't forget to strap in."

There were thirty-two new, undisciplined recruits. Two of them concerned

Radley—a young couple holding hands. The two kissed, and Radley frowned. It was clearly a kiss from love, not lust. What in hell would possess a young couple to travel halfway across the galaxy to risk a horrible death on a radio-active planet?

Radley glared at Wilkinson until he looked. Radley jerked his head towards the couple wordlessly, but after forty-two years working together it was clear what he meant. What the hell is that about?

Wilkinson shook his head and shrugged. Don't ask me; I didn't hire them.

The young man said to the young blonde, "Don't worry, Jessica. After this we—"

"No first names!" Radley snapped, and all thirty-two of the recruits looked at him in shock. "We use last names. It helps professionalism…and keeps you from getting too attached to someone. Only dead men have first names."

Wilkinson spoke up, "Don't worry boys and girls. Listen to us veteran miners and you'll only come back dead in soul." The yellow lights went on, "Now, who's ready to flatline?"

The rookies laughed nervously, but the veterans—except Radley—cheered loudly.

Radley said, "If this is your first jump, I suggest you close your eyes."

"A quick prayer might not hurt either," Wilkenson added.

The green light came on, and Radley blinked. He clutched the bar overhead to regain his balance. "Crew chiefs, check your teams."

They nodded, obviously coming out of the daze quickly. Most of the recruits were simply shaking. Three were crying. One man fell on the ground and vomited.

One recruit glared at the vomiting man and said, "What's your problem? We haven't even jumped yet."

Radley and Wilkinson rushed towards the man and grabbed his arms. Sometimes, only on a first jump, people would not realize they had jumped until a minute or two after. It was a very bad sign. "What the hell are—" was all the man got out before he went into a full seizure. Radley and Wilkinson could barely hold him down. The one on the floor vomiting reached out to grab the convulsing man's feet. Wilkinson tried to stop him, but it was too late. The convulsing man's foot hit the kneeling recruit square in the nose. There was a crunch, and a heavy flow of blood.

Radley swore, and the rest of the recruits kept their distance. Finally, the seizure stopped, and Radley pointed at two recruits. "You two, take him to the infirmary. Tell them he had a jump seizure." He pointed to the man on the floor covered in blood and vomit. "Your nose is broken. If you can walk, go with them."

"Is he going to be okay?" one of the recruits asked.

Veteran miner Pike stepped forward now and barked, "Now is not the time to explain the secrets of flatline seizures. They will both be fine, but they won't make it on this mission. That means you'll have to pick up their slack."

Another veteran, Rede, stepped forward, "And if you want to make it back to this ship alive, I advise you to go check your radiation suits. Those two will get back home alive, but if your suit fails you won't."

Radley was walking away, and Wilkinson called after him, "Radley!"

"No first names, Wilkinson. Call me Radley again and you'll ride home on the outside of the ship."

"Why don't you just send me down to the surface with a short team?" Wilkinson asked.

Radley stopped, "One of those guys is yours?"

"No. Both of them were, so I'm down to you, me and Tristan and Isolde."

"Who?"

"The couple you got mad at earlier," Wilkinson said.

"Why didn't you just say Romeo and Juliet if you were going to be poetic?" Radley asked.

"Because I want them to come back alive," Wilkinson said.

Radley rolled his eyes. Pointing out that Tristan and Isolde also died would be useless. "I'll pull a recruit from some else's team."

Wilkinson shook his head, "There's no reason to send two short teams down like that. Just put my team on scout."

"You're short for scout duty, too."

"Four is the right number for scout duty," Wilkinson said.

"Fine, but you better brief them well. Just make sure they don't try to get 'freaky' on the surface."

Wilkinson shrugged. "I'll get them ready."

Radley moved to the staging area to check his own equipment. A single equipment failure would cost him his life. Beneath the cloth was a layer of fine copper wire mesh that deflected radiation away from the wearer, keeping him or her alive as long as the battery power held. This meant that a miner had eight hours. Crews didn't get much done after eight hours, anyway.

The miners checked their equipment to ensure it was all there. There were axes, crowbars, and other equipment made for smashing and removing wire and support beams. The hand tools would be cast into the smelting pots at the end of the run. In order to save metal, even handles were made from light metals that could be melted down, purified, and recast after decontamination. The heavy equipment was on the surface, and would never leave. It was radioactive now, and too expensive to replace.

The miners were all suited up, and crew chiefs checked their rookies to make certain the suits were worn properly. Radley checked his crew chiefs, and Wilkinson checked Radley. No one, regardless of experience, went to the surface without a check.

The lander disconnected, and slowly dropped into an orbit that would intersect the location of this mining mission. The window spun towards the dead planet below, and the rookie miners—having never seen Earth before—gasped. Sol showed serene blues and greens on the lighted hemisphere. The other hemisphere was in night, and glowed faintly with radioactive decay. You could see the outline of continents glowing against the black seas.

"It looks like back home where the cities light the continents at night," the rookie closest to the window said. "It almost looks inhabited."

"It is inhabited," Radley said. Every one of the rookies looked quickly and expectantly at him. "There are no humans down there, but don't forget about the animals. You have a sidearm for a reason. If you see an animal come towards you—even if it looks like a harmless, cute, baby herbivore—you shoot. Do we know what a deer is?" All the rookies nodded. Some planets had transplanted Earth deer (hunters had made sure that species survived) and others had similar, indigenous creatures called deer. "If you see a baby, there is an adult nearby. A deer's hoof can pierce your suit or break your mask, and if a buck decides to charge, you might end up double dead. There are far more dangerous animals down there, too.

"No mascots, no petting the animals, no feeding the animals. If one comes near you, it's better to shoot first and ask questions later."

The nervous eighteen-year-old with half a beard asked, "Have you actually seen that? The deer attacking someone, I mean?"

Radley was reluctant to talk about Amos. He wasn't afraid of scaring the rookies (that ensured that only the toughest ever returned), but he didn't like remembering the men he had lost. "One of my crew chiefs last trip got too close to one of fawns—that's a baby deer. The buck—a seven pointer—charged head down. It pierced Amos's suit, and—"

"I thought you said no first names," said Ivansky (the boy Wilkinson called Tristan).

"I said only dead men have names," Radley said. "Amos' suit was pierced, and he was bleeding. Then the buck started kicking with its front hooves while he was down. He wasn't able to pull his sidearm to defend himself ... he was dead the moment his suit was pierced, anyway. I shot the buck, but not in time to save Amos."

There was a menacing silence before one of the rookies (clearly the type that felt it was necessary to fill silences with sound) said, "Seven point buck? Did you keep the head?"

"The only thing that comes off the planet is the metal."

"What about Amos?" the same rookie asked.

Radley answered his question with silence.

"Have you lost many men?"

"Mining?" Radley nodded. "Amos, Tyler, Marcus, Preston, Saghira, Jonah, Zachariah, Steve, Oscar, and Bartholomew." The rookies were shocked at his sudden rollcall, and Ivansky mouthed the names silently. He appeared to have an excellent memory.

"So keep your head straight down there so I can forget your name. Understood?" Radley said.

The rookies nodded, but Howell (the blonde girl Wilkinson called Isolde) asked, "Is that a lot? For a foreman I mean. Not that I ... I don't mean to be disrespectful, but I was just wondering if that was normal, or—"

Wilkinson interrupted, "Pond has the best record in the fleet. He's got half as many losses as the next foreman."

It was clear that the rookies wanted to be reassured by this, but were having trouble getting there. Every one of them knew that mining the dead cities of Earth was dangerous when they signed up. It was quite a different thing to be falling towards that danger with a group that considered ten deaths an exceptionally small number.

"Where are we going?" one of the rookies asked. "What city?"

"What the hell does that matter?" crew chief Rede snapped.

"The town we are falling into was called Chernobyl," Wilkinson said. "About six hundred years ago—long before we mastered space flight—a nuclear reactor went critical and caused the town to be evacuated. By the time all the metal ore had been mined and humans were forced to move to the stars, Chernobyl was habitable again.

"Actually, it was more than habitable. It was a veritable paradise for those who stayed behind," Wilkinson said. Chernobyl had abundant animals, undeveloped fields, and fertile, unspoiled soil. It became a very large settlement for the time—about 5,000 inhabitants from what we could tell."

"And then the radiation from the bombs killed them," a rookie said. "I guess you would have hoped that after the first disaster—the reactor—people would have been more careful with nuclear weapons and stuff."

"Son," Wilkinson said, "the only thing that changes throughout history is the names."

"Why did they bomb Earth then?" a rookie asked.

"We bombed it so no one else could use it." Radley said.

"We?" a rookie asked. "Meaning your planet?"

"Meaning the military."

A recruit that hadn't spoken yet asked, "Is it true what people say about Earth? Some people say it's haunted. They say the ghosts of the Earthmen walk the planet. They even say that they can inhabit the animals and use them to kill the humans that killed the Earthmen."

"There are no ghosts on that planet," Radley said.

They came to a relatively soft landing, and the miners piled out. Over the comm system, Radley reminded everyone, "You have eight hours of shielding. Pay attention to your battery meter. When you hit one hour left, stop mining and load up whatever free metal you have. I want everyone back in the lander with twenty minutes to spare. The shielding here is good for a full day, so you're safe once you're inside. Crew chiefs, let's get moving!"

Wilkinson, Howell and Ivansky followed Radley and headed to the perimeter to do checks. After completing a full circle, they stopped at the edge of a wooded area.

"Okay, we've checked for animals nearby, and I don't see any," Radley said. "The ultrasonic speakers on the lander should scare off any new visitors. Part of our job is to look for new areas to mine. Follow me, and stay alert."

"Is it true that if you die here you leave the body?" Howell asked.

"Yes," Radley said.

"But if we can decontaminate things, then why don't we take them up?" she asked.

"Bodies don't melt very well," Radley said.

"Do you at least bury them?"

Radley and Wilkinson did not answer, but she found out soon enough. They had been walking and taking survey notes for nearly an hour when they saw a miner lying in an open field. Wilkinson and Radley slowed, but the two rookies ran towards the man.

"Amos," Radley said quietly.

"Stay back," Wilkinson called.

The suit had tears and brown stains of long-dried blood. The faceplate was broken as well, and it was clear that the suit was mostly empty. Inside the broken faceplate was a human skull.

"We have very limited time here on the surface, and there might be more animals, or buried rocks or metal to pierce suits," Radley said as he walked up. "Digging a grave would take hours, and time is both money and life. If you spend too long doing that, you'll come back short on the haul, or battery power."

The rookies nodded, but seemed mesmerized by the corpse. They had probably never seen a dead man before. After a long pause, Howell bent down and looked at the skull closely. There was a half-inch hole above the left eye socket, and small fractures radiating from it. When she looked up at Radley, she had gone pale.

"Radiation poisoning is a bad way to die. Bleeding out isn't much better. It's better to end it quickly," Radley said.

"Let's move."

"So, I take it you two are an item?" Radley asked.

The youngsters beamed, and Ivansky said proudly, "We're engaged. We hope to raise enough money from this to pay for a really nice wedding."

"I thought the father of the bride did that," Radley said.

"My father died," she said.

"How?"

She looked at the ground. "He was a miner." Radley frowned, trying to remember someone named Howell. "Not with you," she added quickly. "It was a different foreman."

"So what the hell made you think this was a good idea?"

"You can't make money this fast anywhere," Ivansky said.

"Yeah, life insurance pays pretty well to an almost widow. You are both fucking idiots," Radley said matter-of-factly.

The teenagers looked dejected, and Wilkinson said, "You are young and have your whole life ahead of you. So why come here and risk losing it?"

Ivansky squared his shoulders. "My grandfather served in the war. He always said that the problem with kids these days is that there was no military to train them. He said the only way to really have character, discipline, and know who you are is to serve in a war. This was the closest thing around." Radley shook his head slowly. "If your grandfather is still alive when I get back, I'm buying him a drink. Let's go."

After a long walk and another rest, they came upon a small village of houses. Radley pulled the metal detection wand out and motioned for them to follow. They walked in, and Ivansky and Howell drew their sidearms in fear. They waved the barrels recklessly, looking for a target. Radley and Wilkinson gently pushed the teenagers' hands down to a safer direction.

"If you would refrain from pointing that at me ever again, I would appreciate it," Radley said. It wasn't what he wanted to say, but maybe Wilkinson had a point about his temper. There was no reason to startle two trigger-happy recruits anyway.

Wilkinson said in an equally calculated calm voice, "What are you pointing those at?"

"Where the hell are those shadows coming from?" Ivansky asked, shaking with fear.

On the wall were the shadows of three humans frozen in time. Two were adults, and one appeared to be a child. One adult was apparently holding the child to comfort him or her. The other looked like he may have been half turned to shield himself.

It was the heat of the nuclear blast that had made this imprint. Radley had to admit that the positions these three had died in—been vaporized in—was startling. Usually, they were just shapeless blobs, but it was clear that life had been going on as normal only moments before. For lack of a better word, it was haunting.

Wilkinson said, "They're pretty common when you get closer to ground zero."

"But I saw something move," Howell said.

"Me too," Ivansky said.

"Ghosts," Radley told them. "Don't worry; it's just a reaction between the magnetic field and the radiation, or a reflection on your faceplate. Your mind tries to make sense of it, and it makes up ghosts."

"You really don't believe this planet is haunted?"

"Your mind is the only thing that is haunted," Wilkinson said. "It's only natural to feel that way when you're in a planetary tomb."

Radley wasn't sure that was much help, but the veterans went about scanning the walls. The metal content was very low.

The one-hour battery alarms went off, and Radley said, "Let's head back. I didn't realize we had been out so long. It is going to take us at forty minutes to get back. Ivansky, why don't you take care of calling us in? Keep sending reports every ten minutes."

They had been walking for some time when a sudden motion in the bushes caught Wilkinson's attention. A boar exploded out of the bushes behind Ivansky. The animal was nearly eight feet long, four feet high, and probably four hundred pounds. Its tusks were three inches long, and it was charging head-down towards the unwitting teenager.

Wilkinson pushed Ivansky out of the way, but didn't get out of the way himself. The boar hit him in the gut and threw him backwards. Radley drew is pistol, squared up, and fired the entire magazine into the animal's skull. The legs gave out, but the momentum carried the animal forward. Radley and Howell still had to jump to one side to avoid being hit by the carcass.

Sure that the animal was dead, Radley rushed to Wilkinson and surveyed the damage. Wilkinson was still breathing and conscious. He forced the words, "Check … rookies."

Radley sprang to his feet, and grabbed Ivansky roughly. The teenager was frightened, but Radley said nothing as he checked every inch of the suit to make sure there were no tears. Ivansky was okay. Howell had come over, and Radley grabbed her roughly. Radley checked every inch of her suit Howell's suit was fine as well.

Radley knelt over Wilkinson, and the dying man said, "You have to go." Radley shook his head, but Wilkinson was right. He handed Radley his pistol, and said, "Don't leave me like this."

Radley forced himself not to cry as he stood and pointed the pistol at Wilkinson's skull. "Goodbye, Darin," he said as he pulled the trigger.

Radley looked at his battery monitor and saw there was ten minutes left. There was only one problem: it would take fifteen minutes to get to the ship if they ran. Radley looked at the teenagers, and made a decision.

He ripped Darin's battery pack away from his suit, and hooked it up to Howell's suit. She would have twenty minutes now. When Radley hooked his own battery pack to Ivansky's suit, the young man asked, "Where did you get that one?"

Radley lied, and said, "I took it off Amos's suit. We have to run. Once you are in the lift ship the shielding will protect you. Move!"

The three miners sprinted towards the ship, and made it in sixteen minutes. Radley could have made it in twelve alone, but they weren't soldiers. They were just love-struck teenagers who would have long lives ahead of them.

The second the two were inside, Radley ordered, "Close the door!"

The veteran miners moved without asking a single question, but Ivansky and Howell turned in shock. Ivansky saw the empty slot on Radley's suit for the shield battery, and started pounding on the door yelling.

Radley ordered, "Get out of here."

"You have to let him in!" Ivansky yelled. "He saved my life. Let him in."

"Stand down, Ivansky," Radley ordered. "You go marry that girl and stay the hell off of this planet."

Rede and Pike saluted their former Colonel. Ivansky saw this, and saluted as well. Radley saluted back.

"Rede," Radley said. "I don't have any family back home to take care of my estate. Just make sure those kids never see this planet again."

"Understood, Radley."

Ivansky whispered, "Thank you. Thank you, sir." Clearing his throat, the boy said, "Darin, Amos, Tyler, Marcus, Preston, Saghira, Jonah, Zachariah, Steve, Oscar, and Bartholomew ... and Radley."

"Spirits of dead men," Radley replied. "Goodbye, Howell. Goodbye, Ivansky."

"Goodbye, Radley."

The ship lifted off, and Radley removed his helmet and suit. They didn't do much good now anyway. He would die comfortably at least. But before he did that, there was something he had to do. Actually, there were two things. He headed back towards the town center, hoping to find an abandoned shovel. It took him about an hour to dig a grave for Amos, and about two hours to dig a second grave for Darin.

When the Darin's grave was filled in, he sat and rested. Miraculously, there was a bottle of vodka in the house where he found the shovel that had survived the blast. It tasted awful. Vodka did not get better with age or radiation. Radley only had one drink before he gave the majority to his friend. It would probably keep flowers from growing on the grave for years.

Radley looked at the dead boar. It took six shots to the brain and kept coming even after it was dead. That was a worthy opponent. Radley poured the last of the vodka over the boar's head.

He could see ghostly half-shapes of men surrounding the clearing. This time, there was no magnetic field or faceplate to blame. It was far from the first time he had seen the ghosts of Earth, but he never admitted they were more than imagination. How did Darin put it? The ghosts of a haunted mind.

He told himself that radiation poisoning was causing him to hallucinate. After all that work, he was also severely dehydrated. Plus that liquor was probably more poison than anything.

He didn't believe a word of it. He never had. The ghosts now formed a tight circle around him, and he put the barrel of Darin's gun against his temple. He looked into what would be the faces of these men if they were anything more than a failing mind. Before he pulled trigger, he said, "I'm sorry."

Oren Hammerquist is the author of two novels, *Murphy's Second Death* and *Savage Animals*. A collection of short stories will be available this spring from KCL Publishing. He is currently working on a novel prequel to this story tentatively titled *Forging Orion's Spur*. His short stories and poetry have appeared in various publications, and a full list is available is available on his website: www.orenhammerquist.com. Oren is originally from Everett, Washington—just outside Seattle. He has served in the Army for nine years, and is currently residing in Germany. He is happily married with three daughters.

A Life Built on Maladies

by Megan Lee Beals

Mavis was pulling weeds in her tiny garden when the clock in the sky flickered. The hairs perked up on the back of her neck. She stayed her hand and looked up from the barren patch of land she was reclaiming from the crabgrass that plagued her tiny island to scan the horizon for a fire, perhaps a visitor. Then the clock vanished completely and she stared squinting into the sky. Yes, the clock is missing. Soon the panic will set in. She waited, counting the seconds until the clock reappeared. The date read the same as the one in her independent memory banks and under it, in the blank patch of sky left clear for emergency broadcasting, was a message. It was the first written there in over four hundred years: "Remain calm. Crews are working to correct technical difficulties."

She returned to her garden with a savage vigor, pulling out grass as fast as her arthritic hands would allow. Mavis was determined to get at least a full bed weeded before "crews" arrived and begged her to fix the sky. But the weeds were a poor distraction and she could not help but think of the slow disintegration of Heat Sink City that begins with a flickering sky. Almost six seconds had passed without the clock. Her hands locked over a stubborn patch of weeds and she cussed aloud. Six seconds was long enough to threaten the servers that ran the cities; the massive neural playgrounds where most of Heat Sink's citizens lived. If the cities were to falter, the consciousness of the masses would flood into the backup grids—the private quiet places from which she stole patches to create her private island. Soon she would have to share the ocean. Plankton would be the first to go. The ocean could look the same without it, but it made the minnows meaningless. Then the algae would stop growing: it would just exist wherever the programs deigned algae should be. More power would be siphoned away to fuel the cities and the fish would start swimming in recognizable patterns. Their scales would all catch the light the same way, and fishing would be nothing more than a routine.

She did not need to fish for breakfast. Mavis would go on living if she never put another crumb of food in her mouth. But she liked to fish. It was a part of the hard life she created out here on her island. Imperfection was difficult to maintain on the servers. If the cities failed, power would divert to keep the people alive, and imperfection would be lost to glorious mother convenience. Mavis wrenched her hands up and tore the grass from the ground. The little white hair-like roots were still clinging there in the ground in tufts, and if left alone they'd grow back stronger than before. Her hands ached, and for a moment, Mavis was happy.

In the distance a tiny boat bobbed on the waves. She saw it the second it appeared on the horizon. That was pure instinct, not programing. She was an island woman whose eyes were always watching for the warning signs the ocean gives its inhabitants. The fact that he didn't just appear on her front porch--that was programming. In the early days of Heat Sink, anyone with her number could think himself onto her island. She set barriers into its code and stuck her visitors onto a little skerry far enough into the ocean to let her get used to the idea of visitors. Leave an old woman her peace, damn you. Her friends stopped calling, which was all nonsense. She could have just let them swim. Mavis left her garden in its scabby state and walked up to wait for him on her porch. It was probably Jeff. Handsome Jeff with the gray at his temples. Although, last she saw him, Jeff had taken to wearing a younger face. Early college Jeff. She pursed her lips and steeled herself to stare him down with her tired old face and natural nose. He pulled his boat ashore and she let him tie up the boat on his own.

"Apex City is offline, Mave. There's just enough power to run it but we're keeping it down until we figure out what's happened. We've built some holding apartments for the Apex people just outside Shambhala, but they aren't happy."

Mavis' lip curled at the thought of all those pleasure-seekers going an hour without happiness, but she had nothing to say. She put away her disgust, and nodded to Jeff, disinterested.

"Can I get you some coffee, Jeff? I was just going to put on a pot to boil."

He finished tying up the boat and ran up the steps to her porch. "Did you hear me? Apex is down. People are panicking."

"I heard you!" she snapped. He was upsetting the rhythm of her island. He could at least observe the rituals. And he was wearing wrinkles at his eyes again, probably just to appease her. She resisted the urge to sneer at him. Wrinkles should not be a fashion accessory. "Do we have time for coffee?"

Jeff was stricken. It had been years since his last visit. He knew what she was like, but she had made herself such a troll. Her hair was loose and thin, her back crooked, her hands like talons. She was a costume of old age. He shook his head and softened his voice. "I really don't think we do, Mave. We've been working at the problem from all angles, but nothing is wrong on our end. It's an outside problem. We need access to the bots."

She laughed. It was short, and entirely without humor. "I don't want to go outside."

"Billions of lives, Mavis," he shouted. "Yours included!"

She nodded, and forgot about the coffee. She just needed to know she was needed.

Mavis led the way down the path around her tiny cabin to the cellar. With Jeff, the door would not lead to jams and turnips. She opened the door, and they stepped down into a replica of the office she left back in the World. It was longer than the cabin, and the height of the ceiling brought the room far below the water table. The ocean should be knee deep and the bright polished wood floor ruined. The office was impossible, and she hated it. In the center of the office was a 1/8 replica of Heat Sink City with a clever little "you are here" label on the mock server that housed her consciousness. The label was written by a much younger Mavis. She sat down at her desk and turned on the computer. She did not offer a chair to Jeff. There was none to offer. He took offense nonetheless, and sat down on her desk.

"We have to go together, Mavis."

"No." She continued to type. He stopped her hands.

"Please don't make me argue with you."

She glared at him, briefly, to make her position known, then pulled two headsets out of the desk drawer. "I will lead," she said as he took one from her.

"Of course," he said, and pulled the visor down over his eyes.

Mavis hit a key, and two cameras awoke in the outside world, one in his android, one in hers. The cameras panned around the room, but the bodies were motionless.

"Something's wrong," said Jeff. "I can't get my guy to move."

Mavis tried to tap into the twelve other androids, but she could not find any with motion. Three did not have working camera feeds. She looked closer at the room that housed the androids. A fine layer of dust covered every surface, and the papers were all warped from water damage that wreaked its havoc long ago. A coffee cup was next to the keyboard on the desk in the center of the room. The camera zoomed in on its contents. Mold. Mavis shuddered and pulled back from the headset, vanishing that wretched place for the climate controlled office under her virtual island. Jeff flipped up his visor.

"They've abandoned us," he said. Jeff left his place in Mavis' office and cycled through his memory. He came back furious. "We had an account shored up for a thousand years, Mavis. All they had to do was keep the bots in good repair. They killed us, Mavis. We're dead!"

"Quiet!" she barked. Mavis knew the people outside Heat Sink could not be relied on. There were systems in place to keep Heat Sink going long after the outsiders forgot about the city of massive steel monoliths that housed two billion souls. Something must have misfired in the constant updates she was supposed to receive from the sensors outside the box. Perhaps the warnings were rerouted subconsciously as white noise. Perhaps she forgot to manually check on the monitors. For a hundred years. Time was so slippery without the ability to age. Mavis returned to her computer. "I'm going to manually over-write a surveillance drone. We're going to take a look at our city."

"Do you think it will work?"

Mavis stopped scowling at her computer and looked at Jeff. He was anxious, and Mavis saw the great axe of death hanging over him that she refused to acknowledge in herself. She forced some small kindness for him and smiled. "It should. The surveillance bot has very few moving parts. Very little to go wrong." She pushed the visor back to him. "Why don't you ride along?"

He placed the visor over his eyes. Mavis awoke in the surveillance drone, and started its wheels along the hallways of Heat Sink Inc. She still knew the labyrinth of offices and laboratories well. Her consciousness was mapped while she worked there, and the daily walk to her office could never leave her mind. She rolled the bot past her door, long ago sublet to some Roger Dousharm in real estate, and down the hall to the crown jewel of Heat Sink. Her life, her home, and her only refuge. The bot clamped onto the door knob and opened into the housing for Heat Sink City. Grass was growing through the tiles. The glass front of the building was smashed, the metal folded as if the whole pavilion was kneeling, paying homage to the disasters that carried on while the residents of Heat Sink lived in their stainless steel boxes. And even those did not escape the wear of time. "Stainless" was not a guarantee. The steel monoliths were streaked with rust. Mavis trained the camera on the nearest steel housing. The rust was only on the surface. The three inch plate that housed the precious hardware would last indefinitely. The clock may have flickered, but the monoliths were not at fault. She rolled past the first box and stopped at the two in the center of the city. They were tallest, with a wider base and steel five inches thick. These were the places that housed the souls. They had an inverted curve from the base up to their end that was forgone in the others. A slight inversion to give it beauty, to set it apart as a place for human beings. She fought down the idea to inscribe the names of the citizens on its side. It seemed disgraceful at the time. It was enough that the box was curved. She panned the camera around, orienting herself with the remains of the front door. Her mind lived there, about three feet up from the ground, on the south face of the western monolith.

"More rust?" asked Jeff.

"No," said Mavis. "It's nothing. We'd better check the turbines outside."

"Lead on," he said. In the office, she felt his hand cover hers. She slipped away and issued her commands to the surveillance bot. It continued through the wide streets between the high rise banks that contained the algorithms for cities, for oceans and rain. And for her island. The grass grew more thickly as she neared the front door. The tiles were pushed up here; the entrance was being reclaimed by the earth. She found a path through the twisted metal and broken glass to the outdoors.

Heat Sink Inc. was built on a hill, near enough to the city to overlook it, but far enough away to enjoy the lenient building permits of the suburbs. Heat Sink required six wind turbines to power the generators that ran the servers. The turbines were self-repairing, designed to run indefinitely. One of the turbines was not turning.

"No." Jeff whispered the word. Mavis resisted the urge to find his hand and hold him. She shifted the power to the wheels and sped the little bot over to the unmoving turbine on the far side of the hill. She unscrewed the steel plate from the service panel, and checked the screen. It was still operating, and a bright orange alert blared out from the panel. Rod Inoperable. It could mean anything. She cursed.

"We can find someone to repair it," said Jeff. He wasn't convincing. He had seen the same sagging buildings outside Heat Sink Inc. Most without windows.

"Sure." She turned from the turbine and rolled into the street. A single car was on the street. Its tires were deflated and decomposing; the rust had eaten away the paint. Its silver plastic bumper was growing moss. She moved past it without comment and let Jeff draw his own conclusions.

The rest of the neighborhood was abandoned. Bright plastic toys littered the overgrown yards, and grass was growing out from the gutters to retake the streets. She drove to the end of the street without seeing a soul, then started back.

"Don't turn back. We'll find someone," said Jeff.

Mavis continued toward Heat Sink. "The charge is wearing down on this drone. I could take it as far as I'm able, but then we've lost it for good."

"We'll get another bot. Mavis, there has to be someone out there to repair the turbine."

She shook her head, forgetting their eyes were inside the surveillance drone. "Jeff, look." The sun was setting behind the city. There was no motion, no sound, no lights in the high rise buildings. "There is no one to repair the turbines, and our androids are frozen solid."

"We can call someone. Please."

"There's no one to call, Jeff. I checked our contacts. We're alone. If anyone is out there, they aren't picking up their cell phones. We've still got five of six turbines, and the generators are still at ninety percent capacity, even with the cities running."

She docked the bot and they took off their headsets, settling into the solid reality of Mavis' office. Jeff hijacked her keyboard and quickly wrote a cabinet into her office containing a folding chair. He took it out and sat down at her desk, ignoring the glare she gave him. They had more pressing issues than Mavis's stern ideas of world creation etiquette.

"At ninety percent the cities will eventually eat away that reserve power."

Mavis nodded.

"How long until they drain us?"

Mavis calculated the number, frowned at it, then tried some finagling. Jeff coughed in case she forgot he was waiting. She looked up from her figures and laughed. "If we keep Apex offline and run at current capacity, and count on none of the other turbines going down, we've got seventy years. With Apex running at full, we have eleven days."

"And what if we shut down everything? Isolate everyone in the towers? How much time?"

Mavis shrugged. "We're already isolated in the towers, Jeff. They were designed to last forever. They're really just holding tanks for everyone's consciousness. Like a death you could possibly, eventually wake up from."

"And what are the chances of waking?"

Mavis laughed. "Don't ask questions you don't want answers to."

Jeff shook his head. Mavis turned away from him and began to type.

"What are you doing?"

"If we keep Apex down, the people will think we have failed. We gave them four hundred years, Jeff, but they want it to last forever."

"We could shut down all the cities. How long do we have in the back up servers?"

"No. We are cut off. The other turbines will fail. Eventually. We'll have to keep pulling back until Heat Sink is nothing but a huddled mass of fear in a vast white plane of nothingness. I won't have everyone's last days be in fear. We're running full capacity for eleven days, and then everyone in this place is getting pulled to the towers. They won't even know what hit them. It will be a mass sleep. And if anyone is out there to find us, perhaps one day we will wake."

"Mavis, you can't make that decision for everyone."

Her hands shook as she brought up her own code. She lessened the arthritis in her hands, and took the crook from her back. "Eleven days of happiness, or an eternity of fear, Jeff. It's my city. I choose happiness."

He blinked, and her hands were less mottled. The veins weren't knobbed and stretching at her skin. She shut down the computer and folded it down into the desk. "I'm sending out all the surveillance drones as far as they will go. Maybe they will run into someone. They carry a message and instructions for repairing Heat Sink and waking us up."

"And if the drones fail?"

"Four hundred years ago, I inscribed those same instructions in fifty languages. Last thing I did before upload was hang them on the wall of Heat Sink Inc. I didn't think I should worry our customers with the reminder that nothing is forever." She smiled, brightly. "I'm going to make us some coffee now."

She blazed past him and hopped up the stairs into the bright and beautiful summer day. As soon as he joined her on the island, she slammed the door to the cellar and glared at it until she was sure the only thing down there were turnips and jam, then lead the way up to her porch.

"You take it black, I hope? I haven't got any milk or cream."

Jeff stared at her. He had never seen her so happy. "We've only got eleven days left, Mavis. Are you going to spend it all on this island?"

Mavis leaned over and gently kissed his cheek, then casually nodded up to the sky. The clock was still there, and under it was a new message. "Technical issues have been resolved. Have a lovely day. –Management." She watched him read through it, then laughed and went inside. While she ground the coffee, Mavis thought briefly about traveling, then decided against it.

"I'll probably finish up my garden," she called out the window. "Eleven days is plenty time to get my tulips in the ground."

Megan Lee Beals works by day in a bookstore and by night on a novel. In the interim, she knits. Her previous short fiction can be found at *Literary Orphans*, *Luna Station Quarterly*, and in *The Iowa Review*.

The Great Gate

by Alicia Cole

Blue incandescence simmered in the air, electric charge jolting through the circle Peter scrawled on the ground, almost lazily. The bio-feed push-back was tangible: this was top-quality sigilization chalk. In front of the partially completed circle, the Great Gate of Kiev loomed in the dark. Its concrete bulk was veined with steel.

Completing the final arc, all parts of his body carefully inside as the lines connected, Peter crouched in the center. Settling into a half-lotus, Peter connected both of his wrist ports to the holoPad and concentrated on his formula. The device hummed, a faint amber glow flickering across the screen as it communicated with the nanochalk. As he etched symbols across the pad's surface, the chalk circle around him began to shimmer and spark.

Conic energy spiraled up. As Peter continued, his body began to tremble with the effort. Abruptly, the energy cone snapped taut, erupting like a blue trajectory towards the gate.

A horse's hoof, tapping against the metal walkway, woke Peter. With a moan, he shoved his upper body off the hard ground.

The horse's hoof cracked a second time. Peter groaned openly.

A querying, firm voice asked from above, "Où est Dieu m'a amené?"

The young woman, tendrils of brown hair peeking from under her helmet, was fully armored. Her gaze was keen and searching, a soldier on alert.

Peter tapped a finger behind his right ear, surreptitiously. With a soft beep, the translator came online. "You're safe," he assured her, rising slowly to his feet.

Her hazel eyes narrowed. "Only God may tell me so. Where am I? This is not Margny." Then, she paused, the first sign of doubt creasing her face like a scarf waving in the wind. She touched her side gingerly. "There was an arrow from a Burgundian …"

With a rustle of metal, the young warrior drew her sword, brandishing it at Peter's chest. "Are you a spy or a devil? I hear you in my own tongue, but this place is strange."

Peter took a quick step back, his left heel grinding through the chalk circle. Holding up both hands in protest, he exclaimed, "I'm neither, I promise!"

"Can I … your horse …," he gestured vaguely at the empty square and the shadowed gate looming over them, then ran a hand through his dark hair and smiled crookedly. "I'm Peter, Peter Selsko. Will you come with me?"

Her eyes narrowed, her sword at the ready. "Why?"

"I need your help."

The young woman startled, her horse moving uneasily as she turned, looking wildly around.

"They needed me also," her voice hitched. "Did you call me from the battlefield?"

Peter moved to grab the horse's bridle but it reared, nostrils flaring.

Though she paled, the young woman stayed astride. "Are you an angel of the Lord?"

Peter, having moved clear of the horse's hooves, laughed and whirled quickly to show his back. "I have no wings."

When he turned to face her once more, her sword lay across her knees, right hand resting on the pommel.

"Yes, I was sent to you," he said.

She startled, blinked, and quickly sheathed her sword. "Then I will listen to you."

"Joan?"

She touched the cross around her neck and dismounted, handing Peter the reins. "My horse is tired after the battle. Thank you."

"Do you also hear the voices?"

Joan sat in his cramped house, her helmet beside her on the table.

He served tea and she held the cup to her nose, the steam billowing.

"I hear a few," Peter said.

"I have heard them since I was a young child."

Joan turned the cup in her hand and sat it down before running her finger across the length of the metal table.

"Of course the voices are here also." Joan's hand waved absently over her head, encompassing the room and the city beyond. Her breath came, a sigh of relief, and when she smiled, it was the shy smile of a very young woman.

Peter tried to explain, as succinctly as possible. "We are in Russia, in the year 2077."

"Is that so?" Joan laughed, the hard clamor of a church bell.

"Yes, really," Peter continued. "The gate that you came through ... it's a special door. It lets you pass through time."

Her smile, in response, was slightly forced. "The priests would say you know some sorcery. But they said that of me also."

Peter sat, swiveling a chair so that his chin rested on the back and his legs straddled. "That must have been difficult for you."

Joan nodded, her mouth thin while her face composed itself. "It is no matter. At least not now."

Peter reached for her hand, compassionately.

She flinched at his touch.

"Sorry," he said, pulling back quickly.

She took another sip of her tea.

"These voices that you hear, Peter, what do they ask of me?"

In the city center, in a squat building with a gleaming façade, Alexei Gavrikov drummed his fingers on the table. The holo-recording wavered before him.

"Who do you say she is again?" Alexei asked the slender mage standing just behind him, elegant hands clasped behind his back. Alexei's own right hand, rough and strong, kept drumming as he turned to look guardedly at the other man.

"Our best researchers agree. She is a French woman from the early 1400s, Jeanne d'Arc."

Alexei snorted and tapped the recording roughly with his thumb. "Woman you say? A young French girl! Tell me again," Alexei prompted, his eyes narrowing, "why did your order pass this Selsko and why he is working for me?"

The slender man shrugged, almost imperceptibly. "Peter has his uses. His methods may be unique, but his intuition is superb. There are few who can do such conjurings. Joan came out fully formed, without obvious defect. If a bit idealistic and young, he is still a superb magician."

"So you say," Alexei replied dismissively. "Still, I am hiring you, Mr. Gulsef, as well as your errant Cyprian magician. If this young woman is who we need, he's done his job well."

"Selsko will bring her in later today."

Joan laughed. She put both hands on the table and laughed.

At first startled, Peter's expression quickly became perturbed.

Joan kept laughing.

"What exactly is so funny?"

"You want me. Me!" Joan canted her head to the side, her mouth quirked. "To rally your people? For what? So they can," her fingers traveled across the table as she spoke, "march together? For who? To what end? You have no king!"

"I already told you," Peter exploded, "the monarchy was abolished in 1917! The Russian people have been controlled by the consulate for the past fifty years."

"From what you have told me, this consulate is not doing so well. If they merely need a voice, a face, I am not so … willing … as some of the women you have shown me today." She looked distastefully at the holoPad.

Peter reddened. "You are needed for a bit more than that. The people are hungry; they have no faith in the consulate to provide them with bread or truth." He drew his left thumb sharply across the holoPad, punched in a news-feed. Vast farmlands filled the screen, empty save for a few workers with hard faces and harder hands.

"They come to the cities for the money," he explained to Joan. "The farms are left vacant. In the suburbs around Moscow the children are fed protein pellets, grow pale and weak without vegetables while their parents scrape out meager incomes in the technology sector."

The vid flickered, children lined up outside shining buildings. "Our schools are the finest in the world, but the children are taught only circuitry. There is no questioning, no play, no exploration."

Peter ran his hand through his hair, then swiped it across the pad before punching in a complicated numerical passcode. "Surely you know of the Knights Templar?"

"Yes, they were holy men. Martyrs." She shook perceptibly.

"Jacques de Molay, their last Grand Master, founded a separate order before his execution."

A seal, a caduceus surrounded by stars, popped up on the screen.

"We are called the Cyprian Order."

"What do you mean he's late?"

Gavrikov looked up from his afternoon coffee.

"I've scheduled a press conference in an hour!"

"He's not answering my calls," Gulsef said. "Still no Selsko?"

He spoke into the air and a voice from a far-away receptionist answered. "No, sir, he hasn't checked in today."

Gulsef scowled. "My apologies, Lead Consular. I'll find him."

"Cancel the press conference," Gavrikov announced to the air, his coffee splashing as his fist came down with a thud.

Gulsef hurried out of the office.

Traffic was jammed. Taxis and bikes hovered in the early smog.

The movement of a horse and two people, strangely transparent when looked at for too long, went unnoticed on the less traveled walkways below.

Gulsef did notice. His eyes followed a blip on the monitor he held. It moved slowly towards the outskirts of Moscow, away from the cramped living districts to the fields edging the urban sprawl.

He nudged his taxi driver in the right shoulder. "Pull over to that ladder; I'll walk the rest of the way."

Swiping a card, he swung out of the cab and descended, judiciously walking the opposite direction from the moving blip.

As the early light of morning stained the courtyard wall, the door to Peter Selsko's apartment exploded inward.

A man stepped through the gaping hole.

The room was empty. Shards of tea cups littered the floor, blown off the table by the explosion; chairs lay akimbo. The room was otherwise empty.

Gulsef smiled.

Several minutes later, a swarm of well-dressed workers swept through the apartment.

Gulsef ordered, "Collect everything with an Order seal."

☼

"If he runs again, I'm going to fall off!" Peter sat behind Joan, his thighs clenched tightly as the horse rocked forward at a brisk canter.

Precariously, he was seated in reverse, their backs pressed together, facing the horse's rump as he projected a cover. Untrained eyes would see a work cart shambling down the road, pulled by a mule and ridden by a balding farmer. They travelled an old road, still paved in concrete and used by peasantry.

"I promise this will work," he said, clenching his jaw. "Just don't run. We're almost there."

"Do you work for who pays you more?" Joan asked, her voice hitching as the horse's gait suddenly lengthened.

Peter cursed, lurching forward.

"The Cyprian Order works both sides," Peter admitted, breathing heavily and readjusting the projection shield on his wrist. "Historically, we've been more interested in the people's voice, though the establishment doesn't need to know that."

Joan was quiet for a moment. "So, this work on the gate is genuine? You have been looking for someone to speak for the people?"

"Someone like them, yes. Someone not easily controlled."

Joan's hair blew in the wind, a strand sticking in her mouth. She pushed it free.

"I am a peasant."

Then, she laughed, her serious features brightening.

"And only Charles VII could tell me what to do!"

"The Order's government liaison, Gavrikov, agreed that a historical figure would best calm the people. He wanted to drum up patriotism, a renewed trust. We didn't tell him our intentions."

A flash of blue caught his eye, a strip of cloth tied to a low-hanging branch. Beyond, a squat concrete house hunkered into the ground. A tattered jacket, marked with silver branching shapes, was slung over a low wall surrounding the house. "This," he said, tapping Joan on the shoulder, "is where we stop."

"We didn't always have the best of intentions, mind," Peter remarked as Joan dismounted, tying the horse's bridle to a post near the wall. Peter quickly muttered something under his breath and drew a series of three sigils in the air. A hazy shimmer settled on the horse's flanks.

"Anyone who looks will see a stump," he explained, then continued, "We didn't sit down and ponder: how are we going to save the country? It was more to do with saving ourselves."

Joan's displeasure showed on her face.

"It just so happened," a lilting, albeit dry voice, remarked, "you lucked us into something better, eh, Peter?"

Joan spun, on the defensive, while boots crunched their way around the side of the building. Peter smiled. The boots and a hat appeared first, book-ending a body cloaked in drab pants and a workman's olive shirt, all caked in dry dirt, old and weathered. A hand pushed up the brim of the hat, revealing a woman's face. Red hair curled at her rounded cheekbones.

"Vera," Peter responded, moving forward to kiss her cheek. "Nice to see you again."

"You'd see me more often if you came out to the fields, dear," she responded, her voice somewhere between sarcasm and fondness, patting his cheek three times roughly in response.

"And dirty these clothes? I prefer the city, thank you."

Vera tugged her hat back down, shadowing her eyes; they changed from pale blue to a murkier hue as the light dimmed. "Too much metal for me, and too little space. At least the rats have room to move here."

A sour note resounded and the two faced each other silently.

Joan cleared her throat.

"Yes, and this is our friend, then?" Vera turned, businesslike. "The vid came through this morning from the gate."

"My algorithm worked," Peter said, pleased. "And, yes, this is Joan."

"Let's get inside then," Vera responded, opening the door and ushering in the magician and the maid.

Vera laid out cups deftly, pouring a clear liquor from the bottle Peter handed her. "After the road," she advised, pushing stools away from a roughhewn table.

"How's Gulsef?"

Vera turned to Peter.

"Smooth as ever. Gavrikov doesn't expect a thing."

"When did you hear from him last?"

"Day before yesterday."

Vera nodded. "He may have paid you a visit, then."

Peter smacked his forehead and grumbled, announcing to the ceiling, "Don't break any of my teacups, Gulsef!"

Vera laughed, and turned back to Joan.

"As Peter mentioned, we've been working on this endeavor for a while. The forces of knowledge against the forces of darkness! Except," and Vera laughed, "that's really a load of horse shit."

Joan's faced pinched. "Good and evil are not what I would call horse shit."

Vera waved her hand dismissively. "It's all knowledge, just who has the knowledge. There are those among us who will argue both sides."

Joan turned to Peter who gave her a lopsided smile as Vera continued.

"The country's been going to rot for some time. The government controls what goes in, what goes out. Those of us who've studied, those of us who understand what's behind things, have kept our eyes open, but most of the people are blind. They go to work, go home, drink, eat, have more children. They don't understand the writing on the wall so to speak."

Joan's internal battle seemed to still as her face settled into passivity, then understanding. "When I hear the voices, I understand more than others. You hear similar voices."

"Voices that have been apparent for millennia, if you have the ears to listen. Try some."

Vera pointed at Joan's cup.

Joan took a sip and coughed sharply while Peter upended his drink and poured a second.

"This is good for you?" she asked, hitching her breath as her chest shook.

"Takes the dust out of the road," Vera replied with a shrug, mouth quirking. "It grows on you."

Joan sipped again and coughed less sharply the second time.

"It was frightening to me, at first," she said. "Then, I grew to trust the voices. Some were afraid of me because of what I heard."

"It's the same for me," Vera continued. "My parents couldn't understand my natural curiosity, or why I was interested in things outside physical human experience. So many people just don't care."

"We do."

"You believe in God, then?"

Vera exchanged looks with Peter before answering.

"I do not know what to believe sometimes. There is a higher order to things, many of the great thinkers and philosophers believed so."

"The Cyprian Order is more concerned with rational thought."

"Not completely," Peter said. "We have no rules as an order as to belief."

Vera laughed. "No offense, Joan! I think of the voices differently than you."

"There were disbelievers in my time also. We never could agree. But, you and I," she gestured at the two seated at the table, "agree that the people are in need."

Vera stood suddenly and raised her hands wide. "Yes! Think of knowledge like this, as much as your arms can hold! What if people understood more than just a fistful?"

"They might know their own minds as I do."

"What Peter and I have been planning, what the Cyprian Order is behind, is a message to deliver this idea to the people. We're hoping for your help."

"What is the plan, then?"

"You may not have seen them, but in your time you had something called an illuminated manuscript."

Peter pulled out his holoPad and pulled up several images to illustrate.

"They're beautiful!"

"And reverential. They were holy books."

"You don't mean to make one of me, do you?"

"We just need to use your image," Vera responded, a bright note of hope in her voice, "and a lock of hair."

Joan's hand raised to touch her hair as Vera explained, "It's for the work.

We need a biological connection to you to imbue the image with life, make the influence stronger."

"Is this sorcery?"

"It's scientific," Vera said.

"No witchcraft."

"I promise, it's alchemical."

After a moment's consideration, Joan nodded. She reached across the table and took the bottle from Peter before he could refill a third time. Raising her cup, she motioned to Vera to do the same. The pottery clinked.

"A votre santé," Joan said, finally upending her glass.

"Gulsef!"

Snarling, his face red with exertion and frustration, Alexei Gavrikov burst into the dark room. Amid the banks of shining steel monitors, the workers were bathed in a glow of blue lighting. Gulsef looked up sharply from his console.

"Have you seen the news today?" Gavrikov snarled. "She's everywhere!"

He walked to the nearest console, two men hurrying out of his way, and jabbed a thumb at the monitor. A holo-image sprung up. Alexei swiped sideways, flipping through images randomly until he found what he sought. The first image: a library, a feathery series of drawings painted across its left wall, large-scale. The second image: a bank, the same drawings larger over the archway. The third image: an apartment complex, similarly decorated.

A woman on horseback passed through a gate, sketched in startling black. In her open left palm, a silver symbol floated: a wreath of stars with a complicated design of alphanumeric code in the center; in her right hand, she held a golden sword.

"I can't explain it," Gulsef said. "Neither she nor Selsko were found and we removed all of the Cyprian technology from his house. I suppose he could have stolen something from work, but we keep security fairly tight."

"What about your other Order contacts?"

"All accounted for and the ones closest to him properly interviewed. He's left no trace and this Jeanne d'Arc has faded into thin air. Or, into graffiti it seems."

Gavrikov, his brow furrowing, examined the images. "They're not projections," he murmured. "Actual renderings on the walls. Perhaps from some distance. Intricate spell craft … and this …" He gestured at the symbol.

Gulsef examined it, a look of concern settling on his face.

"Viktor," he ordered a short blond man nearby. "Analyze this sigil and quickly. What are we dealing with here?"

The sigil affected the children first. They asked their teachers for books, for maps, for information. The teachers gaped at them, aghast. A few found dusty tomes and handed them out.

Of these, several were immediately fired.

The children kept asking.

It was difficult to track the spread from child to parent, from husband to wife, from friend to friend. There were no riots, only a vague tension building. At play, at school, two camps; in the break room, two opposing sides. For everyone willing to pass a poem along instead of news of the latest vid, another held staunchly to his screen.

"How's it working?"

Vera peeked over Peter's shoulder.

"It's majorly encrypted. One of Gulsef's apprentices, I think."

He punched a few more numbers into place, hummed a perfect D major then leaned in for a retinal scan.

The holoPad chimed an affirmative.

A collection of images sprung up: all the major cities, Joan's image thrown up on building and bridge and factory, a sigil flashing in each outstretched left hand.

"We need to hit these three spots," Peter said while Vera took notes. "Novosibirsk, the new administrative building; Samara's skyway station; and the Leningrad bridge in Omsk."

"And the polls?"

Peter scrolled through several further images, collections of nondescript individuals standing in front of landmarks. A line graph finally popped up.

"The sigil's working! Gavrikov's numbers are dropping. Look at Oskalla."

Vera thrust a fist into the air. "She's a good proletariat candidate! Joan, do you want to see?"

"She's praying," Peter said.

"Oh, sorry. I just got excited."

Peter closed the screens, punching in his own encryption, replete with an F minor.

"Now, about getting her back?"

"I already worked it out."

When the spring elections arrived, Oskalla was elected as Lead Consular, with the Consulate signing a pro-agro bill the same week.

"I've been listening," she announced at her first press conference. "It's time we diversified the work sector. You'll see new classes appearing in the schools this fall, with new jobs arriving in the humanities and sciences."

When asked about the graffiti-spell that was being removed from public view, she merely replied, "The Cyprian Order has that handled."

"Even if I die," Joan said, standing in front of the Great Gate of Kiev, her horse's reins in her hand, "I must return."

Vera's mouth twitched.

"Maybe I can see Domrémy again."

Peter leaned in to kiss her cheek, which she allowed.

"Maybe."

She mounted her horse as Peter ran the new algorithm on his holoPad. Vera readied the chalk circle and both entered.

The sun glinted a brash red on the curves of the gate as Joan rode through.

When she disappeared, the energy dissipating from the two technomages settled into a sizzle on the screen of the pad.

It barely covered Peter's crying.

Much later, the mages would call her the Maid of Moscow. The Cyprian Order released her story in hints and whispers. The flourishing in the nation, an influx of thought that led to a broader renaissance, was attributed to Lead Counsel Oskalla, with Jean d'Arc's image as the people's emblem, representing a resurgence of the arts and sciences, a renewal of interconnected work.

The Great Gate of Kiev remained open; while unused, it became a revered relic sold in miniature to tourists. A statue, a three-dimensional adaptation of the famous image that had swept the nation, was erected in the square.

In the schools it became common to see a holo-glyph of this sculpture near the door: of the gate and of her, leading the people through.

Alicia Cole is an author, editor, and publisher from Atlanta, GA. She works for Studio No. 7 as their Gallery and Membership Coordinator. Her free time is spent in radio theatre and with a household of animals. You can find her fiction in *Issues in Earth Science*, *Torn Pages Anthology*, and *The Martian Wave*. She's the cofounder of Priestess and Hierophant Press, and the author of *Darkly Told: An Audio Chapbook*. Worried she bites? Offer fresh lychee fruit, dark chocolate, coconut water, or good tea when corresponding. Or life stories, ephemera, creative inspiration.

You can find more of her work at www.facebook.com/AliciaColewriter.

Afterword

Please remember that publications such as ours survive on word of mouth. If you enjoy the series, if you find a particular story that resonates, please share that information with your friends, drop a review on Amazon.com and goodreads. Tweet it, blog it, tumble it, reddit, nominate us for awards. It's not enough to read the anthology because you want to be published here someday ("here" won't exist if we don't get more folks reading). There are stories in this collection that deserve wide attention. We work with authors to make that so. It's no accident that *Triangulation: Morning After* received NINE recommendations from Tangent Online's annual recommended reading list. That's nearly half the collection singled out for praise.

David Hartwell describes the small press as the "minor leagues" where authors hone their craft in preparation for major publications. Collections such as ours are useful in working the kinks out of a swing, learning to drive with power, or field your position. We are a stepping stone because we work with authors to improve their craft.

Do you value that? It's really up to you whether we continue.

Steve Ramey, New Castle PA, 2014

www.parsecink.com

www.facebook.com/ParsecInk